"Come away with me. France, Spain, Italy..."

Rebel was so intoxicated with the promise of what she could share with this man, it took her several moments to grasp what was wrong. "Celeste..."

"Forget her!" Hugh commanded.

"I can't!" How could she forget a child who was so much like the lost child she had been?

Hugh cradled her face in his hands. "Let her go, Rebel. She can only come between us."

"Won't you give her a chance, Hugh? Please?" she begged, torn by the dual claims on her heart.

"We can have something, Rebel. You want it as much as I do. Just come away with me—"

"No!" She wrenched out of his grasp. "We can't have anything. Ever. I can't, I won't feel anything for a man who refuses to give a child a chance."

EMMA DARCY nearly became an actress until her fiancé declared he preferred to attend the theater *with* her. She became a wife and mother. Later, she took up oil painting—unsuccessfully, she remarks. Then she tried architecture, designing the family home in New South Wales. Next came romance writing—"the hardest and most challenging of all the activities," she confesses.

Dark Heritage is the second title featuring the James family—Rebel's story. The first was *Ride the Storm*, Harlequin Presents #1401—Tiffany's story.

Books by Emma Darcy

EMMA DARCY

Dark Heritage

Harlequin Books

TORONTO • NEW YORK • LONDON
AMSTERDAM • PARIS • SYDNEY • HAMBURG
STOCKHOLM • ATHENS • TOKYO • MILAN
MADRID • WARSAW • BUDAPEST • AUCKLAND

Harlequin Presents first edition December 1992
ISBN 0-373-11511-3

DARK HERITAGE

CHAPTER ONE

SO THIS WAS IT . . . where it had all begun. Davenport Hall.

Rebel cut the throttle of her hired motor scooter and paused in the middle of the gateway. She gazed down the long avenue of trees to the massive building beyond it. It looked impressively solid and indestructible, proof against the ravages of man and time. Davenport Hall was more than two hundred years old when the first Englishman set foot in Australia in 1770. The thought gave Rebel an odd, eerie feeling.

How many lives had been lived here through the centuries? On any time scale, her mother's brief stay at Davenport Hall would not have measured even the blink of an eyelid. A bare six months. Would anyone remember her, one five-year-old girl amongst forty orphans, refugees from the bombing in London who were later shipped to Australia, away from the bombs and the V2 rockets and the war?

Highly improbable, Rebel thought, that such a transient event forty years ago would be remembered. Even more improbable that one single person of that group would be remembered. Yet now that she had found the place, and given the fortuitous circumstances, it was worth a try.

In the village, Compton Prior, she had been told Davenport Hall was still privately owned by the family whose home it had been for more generations than anyone could recollect. It had been the country seat of umpteen Earls of Stanthorpe.

This titbit of information had given rise to a hope that there might be someone who could remember something about the children if not specifically Valerie Griffith. There might even be some records in the Hall's annals. With so many children, someone must have taken a roll call. At the very minimum, she might be allowed to see the rooms the war orphans had occupied. If anyone could still remember.

For all her life, Davenport Hall had seemed to Rebel like a fantasy, a favourite bedtime story from her early childhood that was probably more dream than fact. Now faced with the impressive reality of the well-maintained estate, she suddenly had a fierce urge to know everything she could find out of what her mother had experienced here, and in later life.

She remembered so little about her. Vague vignettes of being loved and cossetted. Then nothing. After that dreadful interim of homelessness, Rebel's life had been so filled with the James family—her adoptive parents and brothers and sisters—that somehow the past had lost all importance. She had only come looking for Davenport Hall out of idle curiosity, but now the past was here looking at her, beckoning her, and it was irresistible.

Impulsively she switched off the idling engine of the motor scooter. She would satisfy her curiosity about her mother if she could. There was so little to go on, yet any scrap of information would be a feast at a beggar's meal.

Rebel stood up, swung her leg over the seat and pushed the light vehicle off the driveway. She parked it against the high stone wall, which guarded the estate, then unclipped her safety helmet and hung it on the handlebars. Only when she started raking her fingers through her unruly cascade of rich brown curls did she hesitate over the impromptu change of plan. Perhaps she should ring up, make an appointment.

Her original intention had been simply to scooter up and have a look at the place. Now she was here the idea of coming back again seemed pointless, even though she wasn't exactly dressed to impress. Her black leathers were appropriate for riding a motor scooter, and had cost her a lot of hard-earned savings, but the skin-tight pants and battle jacket probably didn't present the kind of image that would get her past the front door of Davenport Hall.

However, the thought of postponing investigation about her mother to some other day did not appeal to Rebel. That was time and energy and money. Anyway, she would only be dealing with servants, and it wasn't as if she didn't know how to sell an idea. She had sold sponsorships and ideas that were a lot more costly and demanding than a simple plea for compassionate understanding. It was definitely worth a try. And if it failed, she would try something else.

Besides, it wasn't as if she looked punk. The wild mop of curls was a natural asset that fashionable hairdressers tried to emulate these days, and Rebel knew from experience she had the kind of face peopl found attractive. It was not an exceptional face but one that was highly individual.

There was nothing particularly noteworthy about most of her features. Her eyebrows were neatly arched, her nose was finely shaped apart from the slight tilt at the end, her mouth was curved as if it was always teetering on a smile, and she had good, straight teeth.

It was her eyes that set her apart. There was something compelling about her eyes. Without any close examination, they were simply bright hazel eyes fringed by thick curly lashes. Rebel never highlighted them with make-up. That detracted from their effect. In fact, the only make-up she wore was lipstick since she had inherited a fine English complexion from her mother, and not even her twenty-four years in the Australian sun had done any damage to it yet.

The only real quarrel Rebel had with her face was the unusual angularity of her jaw line. She would have liked it softer, more rounded, but there was nothing she could do about it except wear her hair long to emphasize her femininity. Not that it mattered a great deal to her anymore. The years had somehow lessened the strong angular effect that had been the bane of her adolescence, or as she had matured and grown to accept herself, the distinctive bone structure simply seemed more a natural part of her. Either way, she was no longer really conscious of it.

Having raked her hair into its usual turbulent cloud, she unzipped the battle jacket to reveal a cherry-red sweater decidedly flattering to her colouring, and of fine quality as well. She used a tissue to dust off her black leather boots, then started the long walk up the gravelled driveway, refusing to feel inhibited or daunted and silently reciting, "Nothing ventured, nothing gained." Even if she was refused admittance to the house she could probably steal around the grounds and imagine where her mother might have played. She wondered if she had been happy in the short time she was here.

Her gaze drifted to the massive trees on either side of her. Their thick trunks suggested that they were as old as the Hall itself. Her mother would have walked down this avenue many times, Rebel thought, perhaps on afternoons such as this, with sunlight dappling the delicate lace work of the foliage.

The leaves were so pretty in their soft light greens, so different to those on Australian trees. Everything in England was different. For the first time Rebel started to comprehend how lost, how displaced her mother must have felt when she arrived in Australia, handed into the care of strangers in a strange land.

Rebel sighed to relieve the sudden tightness in her chest. She knew what it was like to be handed into the care of strangers—the fear, the insecurity. Rebel gave herself a little shake but she could not shrug off the feeling of timelessness as she walked under the ancient trees, the haunting feeling it might have been only yesterday that her mother had been here.

At the end of the avenue the driveway circled a massive stone fountain that must have measured twenty or thirty feet across. Water splashed and tumbled in an endless cascade, soothing, pleasant, mellow. Rebel paused, her view of the old mansion unimpeded by trees.

It was three storeys high, much of its walls covered by ivy. The great rows of mullioned and transomed windows suggested huge rooms within, as befitted a building of this size and age. She could easily see how it housed forty orphans. One room alone may have been big enough for a dormitory.

A little shiver ran down her spine as she stared up at the top row of windows. The air was nippy, despite the afternoon sunshine. And this is what the English call summer, Rebel thought with considerable irony as she forced her feet forward, around the fountain and towards the arched portico that framed the entrance doors.

They looked very forbidding and formidable, those closed doors, but Rebel hastily reminded herself that behind them were people just like herself, no better, no worse, and all she had to do was strike a sympathetic chord with them. To effect that purpose, the first few moments of meeting were critical.

Rebel forced herself to remember her basic training. Stand back. Give the person space to get a good look at you so he or she doesn't feel threatened. Smile. Introduce yourself in a natural, friendly manner. Disarm...

She studied a huge iron doorknocker for several seconds, dismissed its effectiveness in summoning anyone in such an enormous home, then found a modern bellpush to the left of the doors.

It was a minute or two before the bell was answered. Rebel constructed an appealing smile as one of the doors was swung open by a middle-aged woman dressed very neatly in black. Her salt-and-pepper grey hair was permed into a short frizzy cap, and her long face wore a strained, harried look. Housekeeper, Rebel mentally identified her, and instantly injected a persuasive confidence into her voice.

"Good afternoon. My name is Rebel Griffith James, and I—"

"Thank God you're here at last!" It was a heartfelt burst of relief. "We were beginning to think you'd decided not to come, and what we would have done then..." Pale blue eyes were raised to the heavens.

Rebel was momentarily nonplussed by this extraordinary greeting. "You know who I am?" she asked incredulously.

"Oh, yes! The Australian girl," the woman replied so definitely that it left no room for doubt. The door was swung wider and Rebel was gestured inside. "Lord Davenport is waiting for you in the drawing room. I'll take you along to him immediately."

The way was open to her. Although Rebel strongly suspected that some kind of mistake was being made, she decided this was not the time to explain her identity. Opportunity beckoned, and she was not about to look a gift-horse in the mouth. Besides, it was better to address herself to the highest authority in the house, since he would inevitably rule on what she could or could not do.

Her slight hesitation had given the housekeeper enough breathing space to take stock of Rebel's appearance, and already she was looking askance at her black leather attire, maybe having second thoughts about admitting her so readily. Affirm the opportunity, Rebel berated herself.

"Thank you," she said, forcing eye contact. "That's very kind of you. Very efficient. Mrs...?"

The first step in any successful sales pitch was to establish names and memorise them. People responded positively to that courtesy, and it had become second nature to Rebel to get everyone she met onside as quickly as possible. Courtesy didn't cost anything except thoughtfulness, and it invariably earned some consideration.

The woman looked surprised at the question, but the tight worry on her face slid into a slight smile. "Mrs. Tomkins. I daresay we'll get acquainted if you stay long enough. That is if you can force yourself to stay long enough. God knows that no-one has succeeded before, but they do say—" another glance at the black leathers "—that Australians are tougher than most. Hard countries make hard people. I heard that on a television documentary. We all have different ways, don't we?"

Rebel couldn't make much sense out of this spill of words, either, but some kind of reassurance seemed the correct response so she gave it. "Well, I can guarantee that I'll certainly stay here for at least an hour or so, Mrs. Tomkins." Then with all the confidence of having been eagerly—even anxiously—welcomed, Rebel stepped into a huge hallway, as wide as a normal room, its high arched ceiling towering above oak-panelled walls.

The housekeeper seemed to ponder that remark before she closed the door. She turned to Rebel with a sharp measuring look in her pale blue eyes, seemed about to say something more, then apparently decided against it. Rebel wondered if someone in the village had informed the Hall that an Australian woman had been making inquiries. It seemed unlikely that an absolute stranger would be so readily received here, but who or what other Australian woman was expected? Was someone else making inquiries about the war orphans?

Mrs. Tomkins set off down the wide strip of rich red carpet flanked by black and white tiles. Rebel shrugged off the pointless speculation and followed, her glance skimming over the paintings on the walls as they went.

They were all portraits. She wondered if they represented generations of the Davenport family. Then she wondered what it would feel like to be descended from a long line of earls, each member of the family tree known and accounted for over centuries. Did the present earl feel the pressure of his heritage on his shoulders, or did it mean very little to him because he had never known anything else? Could he empathise at all with how she felt with nothing behind her? Her total lack of roots?

The housekeeper suddenly veered right, knocked on a double set of doors and opened one without waiting for any reply.

"The Australian girl is here, m'lord. A Miss James," she announced.

"At last! Wonderful! We might now get some relief. Show her in, Mrs. Tomkins."

The accent was distinctly upper class and had an impatient bite to it. Rebel did not feel encouraged. Nevertheless, there was no turning back now, and she automatically stiffened her spine in readiness for the challenge of winning over a crusty old English lord to her cause.

The housekeeper ushered her into a room of such magnificent proportions that Rebel didn't even see him at first. There were three distinct groupings of chairs and sofas and tables, one directly in front of the largest fireplace Rebel had ever seen, another set close to a bank of six windows at one end of the room. Her gaze finally swung to the other end, the rustle of a newspaper drawing her attention as the sole occupant of the room rose from an armchair.

For several moments they both stood absolutely immobile, staring at each other in surprise. Rebel had never thought of an English earl being much under fifty years of age, but this man looked to be in his early thirties. Not only was he much younger than she had anticipated, but he was also far better looking than she could ever have imagined from the family portraits she had seen on the walls. Refined was the word that came into Rebel's mind.

He was tall and well-proportioned. He wore a classic dark grey suit with an easy grace that made Rebel wonder whether the tailoring enhanced the man or the man enhanced the tailoring. His hair was black, jet black and thick and straight and stylishly cut to frame the strength and the intelligence and the remote fineness of his face. A broad forehead was balanced by a squarish jaw line. Definitive black eyebrows highlighted eyes that were dark and deeply socketed and all the more riveting because of it. A nose that flared with the arrogance of a thoroughbred stallion's. And a perfectly moulded mouth. The lips were not precisely in symmetry, the fuller lower lip showing the curl of sensuality and passion. It was the first part of him to move as it tilted into a mocking, mirthless smile.

"Forgive my rudeness in staring," he said as he started walking towards her. His voice was a deep rich baritone that had no jarring note at all. Smooth velvet. A man who could use the quality of his voice to suggest anything that would give him his own way. "I confess that you don't exactly fit the concept of what I was expecting, Miss James."

Rebel gathered her dazed wits. What had he been expecting? She had no idea. "I need your help," she said, instinctively plucking the line from a textbook situation. It was always a good way to start. People liked being helpful.

His hands lifted in an open gesture. "Anything within reason is yours."

That sounded fine to Rebel. There was nothing at all unreasonable about the request she wanted to make. Maybe he would even escort her through Davenport Hall himself. She was so fascinated by him and the effect he was having on her that the immediacy of wanting to know about her mother had faded into the background.

"That's very generous of you," she said, flashing him a warm smile.

Thick spiky lashes veiled his expression as the dark eyes dropped to her mouth. A weird little flutter attacked Rebel's stomach. Her smile faltered and faded as every nerve end in her body reacted to the tension that suddenly emanated from him.

"Generous..." His voice mocked the word, and the twist of his mouth reinforced the mockery. His gaze fastened on hers, a cynical amusement gleaming a tantalising challenge. "The means to an end, Miss James, and I do hope we can reach a satisfactory end."

"I hope so, too," Rebel murmured, not quite sure what she was agreeing to, and feeling that she was wading into very deep and dangerous waters with this man. Warning bells were going off in her mind, yet the fascination of the unknown had a much stronger pull on her senses.

He waved an invitation to the sofas flanking the fireplace. "Shall we sit down? You can tell me what requirements you'd like me to meet. No doubt you've given the matter some thought."

"Yes. Yes, I have. Thank you."

A warm wave of pleasure washed through Rebel. He was being so accommodating she could hardly believe it. Yet there was a little niggle at the back of her consciousness. She had mentioned the war orphans in the village, but she couldn't understand why both Mrs. Tomkins and Lord Davenport had expressed such relief at her arrival here. There was obviously some explanation. Not that it made any difference now. She was in. And what happened next was of far more importance.

Rebel settled herself on one of the green velvet chesterfields and waited with a growing sense of excitement while her host prodded the logs burning in the fireplace, rearranging them to kindle flames from the red coals underneath. She wondered at the need for a fire in summer, but noted that the action was performed with an aristocratic grace that augmented the charisma of the man.

Sound commonsense cried out that she was crazy to let herself feel so attracted by him. He was a member of the English aristocracy, completely beyond the pale as far as she was concerned. People like him only mixed with their own kind. Yet suddenly she wished life could be different. She wished she had met this man somewhere else, in some other walk of life... on the beach at Bondi, or on a sheep station at Dubbo, or across the room at a party.

He put the poker on its stand and turned to face her. His dark gaze trailed up the long shapeliness of her leather-clad legs, lingered briefly on the thrust of her full breasts, then snapped up to her eyes. Rebel realised, with a heart-hammering little shock, that he was as sexually aware of her as she was of him. A shadow of self-derision flitted across his face before being swallowed into a dark brooding look.

"The child is impossible," he stated, as though it was an undeniable fact that he deeply resented.

Rebel frowned. If he had heard that she had been inquiring about the war orphans, he would surely speak of children, not a singular child. Besides which, her trusty intuition, which had been somewhat fuzzed by the strong attraction of the man, suddenly registered that the vibrations coming from him were all wrong, too deeply personal to be connected to a visit from a stranger passing by.

Something was going on here, something she had inadvertently blundered into. All the same, Lord Davenport obviously needed to be straightened out in more ways than one. If she could be helpful to him, maybe he would more readily overlook the mistake that had clearly been made.

"No child is impossible," Rebel stated with quiet authority. "Some get lost. They can't find the way to—"

"If you cling to such generalisations—however kindly meant—you'll find them sorely tested, Miss James," he broke in, a sharp edge of impatience in his voice. "What kind of experience have you got?"

Rebel summoned all her self-discipline to control her bristling reaction to his condescending arrogance. It was not something she tolerated easily. However, she did her best to present her personal knowledge of the subject, hoping to sort out his problem for him.

"A lifetime of experience," she replied with calm confidence. "My lifetime. That might not amount to very much, but I can only answer truthfully for what I know." She thought of all the children who had been adopted into the James family, most of them traumatised by the raw deal life had handed to them, and how they had all gradually responded to the caring and sharing that became their new way of life.

"There is no such thing as an impossible child," she reiterated, her eyes flashing her firm belief in that truth. "Some have gone down the wrong track. They have problems. Most can be saved. With love and caring. They need to be shown a path that will help them fulfil their own destiny. They need to be motivated. They need to be loved and cherished.''

The dark eyes smouldered at her. ''You take my breath away, Miss James. What sublime tomfoolery—or ignorance!'' he taunted softly. ''And I've always thought of Australians as down-to-earth people who aren't taken in by—what's your word for it? Bull, er, dust?''

Uh-oh! Rebel thought in dismay. Wrong move. She had undoubtedly waded into very touchy waters, and the Earl of Stanthorpe was definitely not in a receptive mood. Best to retreat fast and make her request of him before any harm was done to her cause. She was about to speak up when he corrected his manner, gave her an apologetic little smile and turned his mockery upon himself.

''Please forgive me, Miss James,'' he said with smooth urbanity. ''I am the last person who should be questioning such admirable idealism. I'm grateful for it. I truly am.'' A distinctly unholy challenge gleamed in his eyes as he added, ''Do I understand you're prepared to take the child on, even without seeing her? Even without knowing what she is capable of?''

Rebel took a deep breath. ''Lord Davenport.'' Respectful deference was called for at this point. Not to mention the utmost tact and delicacy. ''I think that you and I both have a slight problem. I only expressed what I hoped would be a helpful point of view. I'm here for a somewhat different reason, I think, than what you suppose.''

"Of course," he said with grim satisfaction. "Much better to drop the pose, Miss James. I appreciate you meant to impress me, but I do prefer honesty. And dealing with reality impresses me far more than mouthing high-sounding principles."

It was not often that Rebel was robbed of speech. On the other hand, it was not often that her integrity was attacked. It took some swallowing. She told herself he must have cause to be so bitter, and it really had nothing to do with her. The situation was getting stickier by the second. The soft answer turneth away wrath, she recited silently, but she wasn't given time to concoct one.

He gave her a sardonic smile. "I assure you, I have no wool over my eyes as far as my niece is concerned. And no doubt the agency briefed you on her infamous record. I accept that negotiations are in order. Some extra inducements to keep you on the job. Just spell them out, Miss James. I'll do all I can to accommodate you. Within reason."

As Rebel digested this last speech, everything he had said since she had entered the room clicked into place. Lord Davenport was looking for a minder for some dreadful, precocious, spoiled wimp of a child. While Rebel was quickly mulling over how best to handle the situation and turn it to her advantage, events were taken completely out of her hands.

The door burst open to admit a little girl who promptly slammed it behind her and leaned against it, her slight chest heaving for breath and her small face set in determined defiance as she glared at the lord of the manor.

That expression was at total variance to the rest of her appearance, which was quite angelic. Her fair hair was like spun silk, falling to her shoulders in a well-cut bob. She wore a beautiful blue dress that would have delighted any little girl's heart. Even the ferocious scowl on her face did not really detract from the delicate perfection of her features. It made the large blue eyes even more vivid.

"Celeste," Lord Davenport ground out in exasperated displeasure. "How many times have I told you—"

"I'm not getting a new nanny!" she hurled at him. Her voice gathered a malevolent triumph as she embellished this theme. "I'm not getting a new nanny at all! Because I just went and got the new nanny and killed her stone-cold dead! So there is no way I'm going to have a new nanny. No way at all!"

CHAPTER TWO

REBEL STARED AT THE CHILD in fascinated horror. For one so young—how old was she, six? seven?—to be so knowingly wicked! Or was the passionate outburst a cry of desperate defiance against crimes committed against her?

Rebel tore her gaze from the child to appraise the man whose authority was being so fiercely flouted. There was no horror, no concern, not the slightest hint of distress at his niece's declaration. His face was a study of cold contempt. He deliberately let the tense silence in the room lengthen and thicken before he spoke, and then it was in a tone of voice that sent a shiver down Rebel's spine. Cold steel, with a silky smooth edge that would slice into the toughest hide.

"Don't lie, Celeste. To prove a murder you have to produce a body. Stone-cold dead. And since Miss James is sitting here, very much alive, we know very well you're lying, don't we?"

Was it a lie, Rebel questioned sharply, watching the defiance on the little girl's face crumple into confusion. Where was the nanny who had been expected? She had obviously been late for her appointment, which was why Rebel had been greeted with relief.

Suddenly the little girl wheeled on Rebel, spitting with furious frustration. "I hate girlfriends! I'll get rid of you, too!" she cried, charging at her with rabid hostility.

Before either Rebel or Lord Davenport could move, Celeste raised her leg and viciously stamped on Rebel's foot.

Years of soaking in her adoptive parents' philosophies went into effect without Rebel consciously thinking. Reacting instinctively, Rebel grabbed the child by the arms and lifted her back as she hitched herself forward on the sofa and pinned Celeste's feet with her booted toes.

"If you're going to be street-wise, kid, there are a couple of fundamental lessons you've got to learn," Rebel shot at her while the little girl was still shocked by the instant retribution. "The first is *never* to start a fight you can't win. With me you can't win, so don't bother fighting."

Respect. Then capture their interest. And after that the loving can start seriously. The memories flooded through Rebel's mind, how each new adopted member of the James family had gradually been persuaded into feeling accepted and loved. Adrenalin spurted through her veins. She could handle this child. All it took was an understanding of what was going through her mind, and Rebel well remembered how she herself had felt all those years ago.

She watched the big blue eyes run through a turbulent range of emotions before frantically falling back on the only attack left to her.

"I hate you!" The lost child's voice shook with the vehemence of desperation.

"That's fine," Rebel returned calmly. "A bit stupid, because all that hatred hurts you more than it hurts me. But if you want to be a lonely loser all your life, you're certainly going the right way about it. A really smart kid would hold back and check out what's best for her before lashing out. Now, are you going to be smart or dumb?"

"I'm smart!" came the furious reply. "I'm a lot smarter than any old nanny."

"Fine. It just so happens that I'm not a nanny. So back off, kid, and don't tread on my toes again. When it comes to toe crushing, I can beat you hollow."

Rebel lifted the pinning pressure of her boots then released her grip on the child's arms.

Celeste hastily stepped out of reach. She shot a look of panicky appeal at her uncle. Whether he might have come to his niece's support was a moot point, but it was readily apparent that he was too stunned by the fast and unexpected turn of events to even raise an eyebrow.

"I'm not frightened of you," Celeste fired at Rebel, reverting to mutinous defiance.

Rebel sat back and gave her a slow, approving smile. "That makes two of us, kid. I'm not frightened of you, either."

"Stop calling me kid!" The blue eyes flashed with aristocratic pride. "I am Lady Celeste Davenport!"

"Huh!" Rebel scoffed. "You're not a lady. You're only a kid. In fact, a gutter kid. They're the only ones who beat up on nannies and leave them stone-cold dead.''

The blue eyes narrowed in appraisal. A quick decision was made. "I didn't beat her up," came the petulant denial. "I didn't kill her, either. I could have killed her if I wanted to, but I only locked her up in the gazebo. So I'm not a gutter kid.''

Rebel breathed a sigh of relief and turned her gaze to Lord Davenport who still stood in front of the fireplace. The dark eyes locked onto hers, full of searing questions.

Rebel shrugged. "First things first, m'lord. You have a nanny to rescue from the gazebo," she pointed out calmly. "You can safely leave your niece with me. If she doesn't beat up on me, I won't beat up on her.'' She swung her gaze to the child. "Bargain, kid?''

"Stop calling me kid!''

"Then sit down and act like a lady. If you can.''

The blue eyes ran scornfully down Rebel's black leather outfit. "You're no lady!''

"I don't pretend to be. But I'm doing a better job of acting like one than you are. And you'll never know who you are or what I am unless you sit down and start acting as smart as you think you are.''

"I've got nothing to learn from you.''

"Yes, you have. For one thing I can teach you how to be a good fighter. And unless you're a good fighter, you just keep getting beaten all the time.''

Rebel saw it then, the first flicker of interest. She'd got through to Celeste. How many times in her life had it been as hard as this ... five, six, seven? A tough one to crack with the resistance running so deep, but the hook was in, and Celeste was not about to back off.

"I'm going to sit over there because I want to," she asserted.

"Fine, kid. You do whatever you like," Rebel returned carelessly.

She flounced onto the sofa opposite Rebel, her eyes filled with hatred but her face set in belligerent determination to prove she was smarter than her antagonist.

Rebel raised a quizzical eyebrow at Lord Davenport, who still hadn't moved. "The nanny?" she prompted.

"Miss James," he bit out savagely, then his lips compressed over the outrage he was clearly feeling at her abrogation of his authority. "I'll have quite a lot to say to you on my return. And to you, also, Celeste," he added, stabbing a look of bitter distaste at both of them. His anger hung in the room even after the solid oak door was closed firmly behind him.

Rebel ruefully figured he wouldn't be satisfied with anything less than a Spanish inquisition on her once he had dispensed with his niece. His pride had taken a severe dent. But as Rebel turned her gaze to the child sitting opposite her, she had no regrets whatsoever about what she had done. It could hardly be described as an exercise in upper-class refinement, but it had been effective. And it was this little girl who carried the far deeper hurt.

"I don't care what he says!" Celeste burst out belligerently. "I hate him. I hate everyone."

It was a cry that echoed out of Rebel's past, and the memory came back sharp and clear. It was after her mother had died, after she had run away from that awful foster home and been drawn into the midst of the James family. Despite their kindness, she couldn't bring herself to believe in it. She had felt so lonely and frightened for so long, she had lashed out indiscriminately, wanting to hurt because she hurt so badly herself, convinced that no-one really wanted her.

"Where are your parents?" she asked, curious to know the little girl's family background.

"They're dead," came the blunt reply. "And he has to look after me."

"I'm sure he wants to look after you."

"No, he doesn't. He doesn't want me at all. He doesn't like me. That's why he keeps getting nannies, so he can stay away and not take any notice of me."

"I see. So you kill the nannies stone-cold dead to make him take notice of you," Rebel said softly.

Celeste instantly bristled with rejection. "I do not! I do it because nannies are old goats. He doesn't care about me, and I don't care about him, and you don't know anything!"

Rebel recalled having said something like that to Zachary Lee, her big, gentle brother from America who had always turned her wild wrath away with kindness and compassionate understanding. Celeste needed a Zachary Lee. The only problem was that people like Zachary Lee James were not exactly thick on the ground. It was a pity Celeste couldn't be adopted by the James family and given the warm sense of belonging she obviously didn't feel here at Davenport Hall.

Rebel's heart went out to her. Couldn't her uncle see Celeste was starved for real affection and caring? That her sheer ferocity was a deep inner cry of anguish at not belonging to anyone? That a hired nanny could never supply what she so desperately wanted?

The problem and its solution seemed so clear to Rebel.

Something ought to be done about it.

Yet what could she do? As it was, she was not about to be thanked for interfering in private family business.

"Who are you, anyway?" Celeste demanded. "You said you'd tell me who you are."

It was the second hint of interest that was not wholly centred on herself. Rebel smiled. "Just a visitor. A long time ago, there was another little girl who came to stay here. She was like you because she had lost her parents, too. That girl was my mother. She didn't have an uncle to look after her, or anyone who could afford to get her a nanny, so other people put her on a boat. That's what they did in those days. They sent orphans halfway around the world to Australia. She never saw England or Davenport Hall again. But she always remembered it. She said it was beautiful. She died when I was about your age. I made up my mind that I would come here one day and see what she had seen. And this is the day."

"Did she have my room?" Celeste asked, reluctantly intrigued by the story.

"I don't know. I wouldn't think so. There were forty orphans here all together. My mother was just one of them. I remember her talking about Davenport Hall, but I don't remember much else about her. Do you remember your parents?"

"'Course I do!" The petulant look came back. "They always got me nannies, too. I don't care that they're dead. I'm glad. Because my mother never told me stories. Uncle Hugh doesn't, either. He's just like them. He goes away all the time and leaves me here."

Rebel's heart gave another lurch. She had heard that *cri de coeur* too many times in the past. She wished she could do something about it, yet she was committed at the present moment. She had to deliver the sponsors for the big charity race her brother had organised. Zachary Lee trusted her to do that, and no way was she going to let him down. Besides, all the balloonists they had lined up were also counting on her ability to sell the idea. She couldn't let any of them down.

She could only spread herself around so far before her effectiveness started to get blunted. She prided herself on delivering what she promised with a totally committed backup. How could she possibly get involved here?

Rebel's train of thought was broken by Celeste, who had obviously decided it was time to take the initiative.

"I don't like you calling me kid," she said, eyeing Rebel in fierce challenge.

"When you earn my respect, I'll call you Celeste. Not before, though."

A gleam of calculation altered her expression. "What's your name?"

"Rebel. Rebel Griffith James."

She wrinkled her nose. "What kind of name is that?"

"Mine."

The answer didn't satisfy. "Why are you wearing those clothes? Are you a criminal? Or are you are a bikie?"

"Neither. These clothes were the most suitable gear I own for riding down from London on a motor scooter. Which is what I did today. But I've ridden bikes, too." Rebel offered her a friendly smile. "What I like best, though, is going up in a balloon."

"A hot-air balloon?" Another gleam of interest. "You mean like in *Around the World in Eighty Days?*"

"Uh-huh. Best way to travel. It's so quiet and beautiful sailing across the sky. A friend of mine is doing balloon trips in the south of England. I'm going to see some of the countryside that way."

"I wish I could," Celeste said glumly.

"Why don't you ask your uncle?"

"He wouldn't let me. He hates me."

He picked that moment to enter the room, freezing the meagre amount of warmth that Rebel had managed to kindle. Remote and unreachable, Rebel thought, her heart sinking at the inflexible stance he took as he addressed his niece.

"Go to your room, Celeste. And don't leave it before I come to you."

Each word an icy rebuke, an icy rejection of all that Celeste was. The little girl's shoulders slumped as she gracelessly worked her way off the sofa and stood up.

"Hey!" Rebel said softly. "It was a pleasure meeting you."

The head lifted, a blur of desperation in the blue eyes as they sought to assess whether Rebel really meant it or whether it was another adult lie.

Rebel's mind screamed, "Reinforce the message. Don't let this opportunity slip away." "You've got potential, kid. Real potential. You could be a great fighter one day. I hope you make it."

The head dropped down. There was no reply. She trudged across the room to the open door. She didn't look at her uncle. Just before she stepped into the hallway, she stopped and looked at Rebel, the big blue eyes awash with tears.

"I wish I had a mother like you, Rebel," she said haltingly.

"Celeste!" Another icy rebuke from her uncle.

The little girl's face contorted as she lifted her eyes to the man towering above her. "I hate you! You never care! You never care!" she sobbed, and ran into the hallway.

Rebel was on her feet before she even thought about what she was doing, every compassionate instinct she had urging her to go after the child, to comfort her and assure her that somebody did care.

"Stay right where you are, Miss James."

The order cracked across the room like a whip, stopping her in her tracks. Rebel glared her own icy rebuke at him as he closed the door and stood guard in front of it.

"You really don't care, do you?" she accused.

His arrogant mask of superiority slipped. The deep inner fire of passion blazed from his eyes. "My feelings, or lack of them, are not your concern. Don't involve yourself in something you know nothing about. Nothing!"

But Rebel's blood was well and truly up, and she wasn't going to let him evade the issue. "I don't like your attitude with the child. You're doing so much damage..."

"I will not tolerate tantrums, Miss James. Discipline breeds character. We've had five hundred years' experience of it, and not without some success," he returned with haughty condescension.

"Not in this case, Lord Davenport," Rebel returned hotly. "I'd say it's the worst kind of failure. Totally negative and destructive. Just how long has your niece been in your care?"

"That is none of your business, Miss James," he bit out angrily.

"It's a measure of the damage you've done with your brand of discipline!" Rebel shot at him. "Are you always so heartless? So lacking in perception?"

For a moment he seemed nonplussed by the attack on his character. He frowned, clearly unsettled by this description of himself. Then the dark eyes stabbed at Rebel, smouldering with dislike and resentment at her effrontery.

"I do not care for the way you handled the situation!" he snapped. "And it certainly showed your earlier hypocrisy in talking about loving and cherishing."

Rebel's eyes burned with scorn. "It's obvious that you don't know the first thing about children. At least I earned her respect. And that, Lord Davenport, is what you've got to earn from her—not insist upon, but earn—before you can even begin to heal the hurts that child has suffered. Then, and only then, might she begin to believe in loving and cherishing and come to accept it."

To punch home the point, Rebel added, "The position and power that your title and wealth give you might command a superficial respect. No doubt you're used to people bowing and scraping because of a heritage you were born to. Born to, not earned. But it's how you treat people that earns deep-down respect. Overbearing authority will only ever stir rebellion."

His eyes flared with a proud contempt for her opinion. "No doubt you have a different point of view to mine. But I am not in the habit of resorting to physical violence, Miss James, however deeply provoked I am. Nor will I permit it."

Rebel stood her ground. "I did no harm, Lord Davenport. That child knows precisely where she stands with me. Like it or not, that's a good feeling. A secure feeling. It's not knowing that's so unsettling and scary."

"You seem to know a great deal, Miss James." He strolled away from the door, directly towards her, a dark menace in every step. "You have the advantage of me. You enter my home somewhat deceitfully—"

"I did not!" Rebel cut in forcefully, ignoring the wild skittering of her pulse. "I had no sooner started to introduce myself than Mrs. Tomkins welcomed me and hurried me into your presence. None of this was my fault. When I realized a mistake had been made, I tried to correct you. You wouldn't be corrected. It's all your fault. And we were interrupted before I could straighten you out completely."

"Then straighten me out now, Miss James. Who and what are you?"

He halted a bare foot away from her, forcing her to look up at him.

Rebel refused to be intimidated, even though his closeness was playing havoc with her stomach. She had never before taken a backward step in her life and she wasn't about to now. She held his gaze unwaveringly, questioning the disturbing effect he had on her, wondering about the heart of the man and why he couldn't perceive the terrible insecurity of the child in his care.

"I am," she said slowly, "no matter how much you dislike it, no matter how much you resent it, the woman you're going to employ to look after your niece. That, Lord Davenport, is who I am."

She had done it now!

Plunging straight into a situation where even the most intrepid angels might fear to tread!

Yet what else could she have done? Rebel had never felt so needed as she was needed here. Somehow she was going to have to juggle things to make enough time for everything. But more than anything else, she had to make some real quality time to help that desperately lost little girl.

Lord Davenport looked down at her with a volatile mixture of incredulity and contempt. "I have never encountered such unsurpassable arrogance. You really take my breath away, Miss James."

"The way you've behaved this afternoon has done exactly the same thing to me," she retorted sharply, not budging an inch. "In fact, I'm battling to get any air into my lungs at all."

His eyes glittered with danger signals. "And if I refuse to employ you?" he asked silkily, obviously anticipating some form of self-seeking retaliation and waiting to pounce if her reply gave him any grounds at all.

"The child's welfare is the only consideration," she asserted firmly. "And that is of paramount importance. In all conscience, Lord Davenport, you can't refuse your niece a chance of turning away from the totally self-destructive course she has taken. I can give her that chance."

Rebel paused, then with her own sting of contempt, added, "Unless, of course, you have no conscience where she is concerned. Unless you truly do hate her."

His face tightened. His mouth thinned into a savage little grimace as he stepped away from her and paced slowly behind the sofa where Celeste had sat. One hand gripped the velvet backrest, fingers digging into the soft pile as he stopped and stared into the fire, which had burnt low again. The tension emanating from him was strong enough to stretch Rebel's nerves taut. It made her wonder if he did hate his niece, if he would prefer to see her damned rather than saved. It was a very disquieting thought.

"I know nothing about you," he bit out, his face still half-averted from her.

"You heard your niece. She could not have given a more positive response to me. What more do you need to know?" Rebel challenged.

"Your background." He swung around and shot a scathing look down her black leather gear, dropping pointedly to her booted toes before slicing back up to her face. "What would I be inviting into my home, Miss James? A street-wise woman who knows how to fight?"

Rebel burned. And completely lost her cool. "Better that than a fool," she flared at him. "Or a wimp. Or a narrow-minded person like you, Lord Davenport, who sees only one way of doing things even when it's proved a total failure."

"You are insolent!"

"And you are insulting!"

"The way you acted with my niece—"

"Was one of the best sales pitches I've ever made. That happens to be my expertise, Lord Davenport, selling. And that doesn't include my body."

"Selling." His mouth curled. "So you chalked up another triumph. My niece thought you cared about her."

Rebel only just pulled herself back from the brink of flying at him tooth and claw. She could not remember the last time anyone had riled her so much. It took all her willpower to control the primitive im-

pulses he had stirred and force a measured pace of
authority into her voice.

"You don't know much about selling, do you? Unless you really care, Lord Davenport, you fall flat on
your face. Insincerity or half-heartedness will cut you
out before you've even started. To satisfy all parties
you need negotiating skills that require the utmost attention to every detail and to every nuance of need.
And the final proof of caring is the backup you deliver. And the sincerity with which it is given."

She paused to draw breath. "It's not going to be
easy for me to fit my other commitments around
looking after your niece, Lord Davenport. You're going to have to help me. But I care enough about that
little girl to give her the best backup and care and
support I can. The only question is, do you care
enough to accommodate my needs?"

His eyes narrowed. "Which are?"

Rebel's mind swiftly ran over her program for the
weeks ahead and sifted out the necessities. "I'll need
a car at my disposal. I'll have to have free use of your
telephone to make whatever calls I need to make, and
a fair proportion of them will be international. I've
given people my Mayfair address, so that will have to
be substituted . . ."

"Mayfair!"

His surprise that she had an address in one of the
most prestigious parts of London gave Rebel an almost malicious pleasure. She could have told him that
the house belonged to her brother-in-law, that it was
one of Joel Faber's many kindnesses to the James
family that each and every one of them had an open

invitation to stay, or make use of, any of the properties owned by him or his multinational organisation. But such an explanation would undoubtedly make this man think she was a freeloader, and she had had enough of his assumptions about her.

"Yes," she said in proud challenge. "That's where I've been staying since I arrived in England. Where I intended to stay for the duration of my visit here. Does that make me respectable enough for you, my lord?"

She gave the address form a biting edge of mockery. He was certainly not her lord nor master, and the urge to smash his monumental air of superiority was gathering force by the moment, overwhelming her usual good sense of discretion.

He breathed in hard and wiped all expression from his face. "Just who are you, Miss James?" he demanded tightly.

Something inside her head snapped, and Rebel's much-prided self-discipline took wing and flew out the window. Pure and utter sauce dripped off her tongue.

"I'm precisely who you thought I was, my lord. An Australian. One of those down-to-earth people who aren't taken in by bulldust. Particularly of the upper-crust variety!"

No sooner were the words out than the sane part of Rebel's mind recoiled in horror. She had completely blown any advantage she had won. No point in arguing that it was his fault for being such a lordly beast. She should have risen above that and kept her priorities in order. It wouldn't be she who suffered for her loss of control, but the child who needed her help.

As she struggled to gather wits enough to counter the stupid self-indulgence, her eyes registered a strange metamorphosis on Lord Davenport's face. The tightness disappeared. His mouth loosened up and started to twitch. The dark eyes were suddenly lit with some wild, unholy joy. Then, to confuse her even further, he threw back his head and laughed outright, a veritable shout of full-blooded laughter that echoed around the huge room, dispelling all the bitter tension that had swirled between them.

Rebel stared at him, any possible train of thought completely shot to pieces. She was vaguely aware that her heart was thumping quite chaotically. However much of a lordly beast the Earl of Stanthorpe was, he looked devastatingly attractive in this lighter mood, and when he stopped laughing and swept her with a twinkling look of approval, her stomach positively flipped.

"Miss James—" his voice purred her name "—I humbly beg your pardon for my crass reaction to a situation that caught me unprepared and out of humour. Clearly you are a woman of unshakeable strength of character." He smiled. "And very possibly a match for Celeste."

There was something not quite right about that smile, but Rebel couldn't define what it was.

"It's extraordinarily generous of you to offer your time and expertise as you have," he continued in that caressing purr custom designed to smooth ruffled feathers. "And your compassion for my, uh, troubled niece does you endless credit. Please—" he waved a graceful invitation to the sofa she had vacated

"—won't you sit down again? I'll ring for afternoon tea. Then perhaps we can start all over. And reach a better understanding."

Rebel finally got her tongue to work. "Thank you. I'd like that," she said stiffly.

It was crazy, she thought, to feel so uneasy. Yet as she sat down and watched the Earl of Stanthorpe deliver his instructions for the serving of afternoon tea over a house intercom, all Rebel's well-honed antennae for trouble were quivering uncertainly.

The sudden volte-face from Lord Davenport should have been a relief.

But it wasn't.

Rebel wrenched her gaze away from the man, needing some respite from the disturbing chemistry he stirred in her. Her eyes drifted around the elegant room. It represented centuries-old wealth, the ultimate in refined and enlightened civilisation. So why did she sense something dark lurking in this heritage?

Something dark in Lord Davenport's about-face.

Something dark in his smile.

Why did she suddenly feel a web winding around her, drawing her into something she should have no business with at all?

CHAPTER THREE

STAY COOL, calm and collected, Rebel instructed herself sternly as Lord Davenport settled on the sofa opposite her. There was a little girl who needed her help. That was perfectly clear-cut. To let herself get muddled by strange feelings was counterproductive to her aim. The battle had been won. All she had to do now was settle appropriate arrangements with the man who had conceded to her interest in his niece.

His tall, lean body folded into a relaxed pose that mocked her own tautly strung nerves. He offered her a whimsical smile, appealing for a lightening of her humor. The dark eyes projected a wealth of warm approval that made Rebel feel even more uneasy. Despite all her experience, she could not place this man in some familiar pigeonhole. And he was so disturbingly handsome it kept tipping Rebel off balance.

"You're right, Miss James," he purred, clearly intent on pouring oil on troubled waters. "Celeste must have our first consideration. I apologise for not fully appreciating the point you made earlier about my niece's positive response to you. That, in itself, is so remarkable it should have given me pause for thought. The child invariably hates everyone. Yet you managed to turn her around, which is no small tour de force. I salute you for it. I'm sure Celeste will benefit greatly from having you as her nanny.''

Very, very smooth.

Rebel mentally applauded the tactic of icing the cake with so many compliments to her as he drove towards his end purpose. A nanny for his niece. Someone to give him and the rest of his household relief. Rebel wondered if he had been laughing at himself for having been such a fool as to even question the opportunity of having the position filled. That would certainly account for the abrupt change of manner.

The battle was not won at all. It was about to shift to new ground. But this time, Rebel vowed, she was not going to lose her temper. She smiled, her eyes projecting a rueful appeal.

''I'm afraid you have misunderstood me again, my lord,'' she said on a wry note. ''I was not offering myself as a nanny. Your niece hates nannies, so such a move would be instantly counterproductive to any progress with her. Apart from which, I have business commitments that preclude my filling the role you would expect of a nanny.''

The warmth promptly faded as he realised he was not about to get his own way. An aristocratic reserve set in as he remeasured Rebel's mettle. ''What precisely are you offering, Miss James?'' he asked warily. ''If my recollection serves me correctly, you said you wanted me to employ you to look after my niece.''

''Employ in the sense, make use of,'' Rebel answered with slow, deliberate emphasis so that it sank in beyond any possible misunderstanding. ''I have considerable experience that you can employ on Celeste's behalf, my lord. But in the sense of being your employee, bought and paid for and beholden to you or your opinion or your requirements—quite simply, that is not what I'm about.''

The aristocratic reserve became even more pronounced. The dark eyes glittered with suspicion. ''I would like to hear what you *are* about, Miss James,'' he stated coldly.

This was the crunch. Make or break time. Rebel had no illusions about what was at stake.

''I wish I could give your niece my full attention, my lord,'' she began quietly. ''She needs a guiding hand very badly. What I'm offering is all the time I can give her, and for that I need your cooperation in setting up a situation that she will find acceptable.''

Suspicion receded. A hard watchfulness took over. ''Go on,'' he invited non-committally.

Encouraged, Rebel mentally skimmed through her own situation. ''It's best if we act as quickly as possible, while the impression I made on your niece is still fresh in her mind. I need to return to London to make necessary arrangements but I'll have everything cleared by tomorrow morning. In the meantime, it would help a lot if you tell Celeste that you've asked me to stay at Davenport Hall while I'm in England because you do care about her and you thought she might like to have me here.''

''I see.'' His mouth took on a sardonic curl. ''You want to move into Davenport Hall as my guest. For an open-ended length of time.''

Rebel ignored the cynical interpretation of her proposal, although she resented the implication that she was some kind of social-climbing parasite or an opportunist who would use a child's need to feather her own nest. She had to keep the argument focused on Celeste and subtly apply enough pressure to force her adversary's hand.

"As a guest I'm no threat to your niece, my lord," she explained. "She has the choice of accepting my company or avoiding it."

"Supposing she avoids it?" he asked silkily, his eyes mocking her theory. "You won't be doing much looking after her if she chooses to keep away from you."

Rebel smiled, fairly confident that that would not be the case. "I'll strike a deal with you, Lord Davenport. Give me a week here. If Celeste avoids my company more than she seeks it during that time, I'll accept that I cannot reach her, and you will be relieved of me as a guest. Does that put you more at ease with my proposal?"

One eyebrow lifted in quizzical challenge. "Only a week, Miss James? You're gambling on long odds. What makes you think you can win?"

"Experience."

"Ah, yes." Again came that smile that held something dark. "I was forgetting that selling is very much a confidence game."

"Which has to be matched to integrity, my lord," Rebel sharply reminded him. "Promising without delivering is ultimately a loser's game. It certainly won't work with your niece."

The smile twisted into a grimace. "I doubt that anything will work with my niece, Miss James. As for the deal you offer, it's not what I had in mind for her."

"What you had in mind, my lord, has just been scuttled, has it not?" Rebel swiftly interjected. "You would not have been offering me the position of nanny if the one Celeste locked in the gazebo was still waiting in the wings. You haven't got a nanny for her, and from what you've told me, it won't be an easy matter to get one. A few more days, a week... What have you got to lose by trying my deal?"

He frowned, unable to refute her argument.

"At least your niece will get part-time care from me while you arrange something more to your liking," Rebel said smoothly. "And should I prove successful in changing her behaviour for the better, you'll have a bonus result, wouldn't you say?"

The dark eyes sliced at her, hard and probing. "You mentioned other commitments, Miss James. The need for a car at your disposal. Freedom of communication. I'd like to know precisely what business you are involved with."

"Of course," she agreed, giving him another smile to show she understood his natural concern about what he would be inviting if he accepted her as a guest. "I'm here in England to find sponsors for one of the most spectacular charity events ever organized. You may have read about it. One hundred and fifty balloons starting off in England and travelling right across Europe. The greatest balloon race in history."

"I saw a clip about it on television," he said, his expression sliding to one of wary reserve again. "You're involved in selling the sponsorships?"

She nodded. "That's my job. The sponsor puts up twenty-five thousand pounds. In return, he gets prestige, excitement and a huge advertisement for whatever he wants to advertise on his balloon. The race will be featured on television every night, giving wide coverage to the sponsor's product. The winner nominates the charity to benefit. I've based part of my selling strategy on promoting competition within competition, so to speak. For instance, I've already signed up every major brand of beer in the world. This makes for extra interest amongst those parties involved."

His eyebrows lifted in appreciation. "Impressive! How far down the track are you in getting the numbers?"

"One hundred and seventeen already signed. Another thirty-three to go."

"You're one of a team in this part of the enterprise?"

Rebel couldn't stifle a grin. "I'm it, my lord. No-one else. It's entirely up to me to deliver the sponsors, on time and all accounted for. I have earned a reputation for delivering what I promise," she added for good measure.

The dawning look of respect on his face was soothing balm for all she had swallowed from him. It also boosted her confidence. He could not dismiss her claims quite so easily now.

"That's quite a responsibility for one so young," he said questioningly.

Rebel shrugged. "Young in years, perhaps, but not young in this field."

He shook his head. His mouth curled in ironic musing. "You are a surprise package in more ways than one, Miss James."

Rebel relaxed enough to laugh. "You were quite a surprise yourself, my lord. My mental image of English earls was of more elderly gentlemen."

The dark eyes flashed with dry mockery. "As you so pointedly stated, that is a matter of heritage. Not earned, and not impressive." His mouth twitched with some inner amusement. "At least, not to an Australian."

"Oh, I wouldn't make that generalisation, my lord," Rebel said with a wide grin. Her eyes danced teasingly, encouraging more good humour to shift the ground even more her way. "Lots of people are impressed by titles. I'm just not one of them. And that's a matter of my particular heritage."

"Which is?" he asked with a definite sparkle of interest.

"I have none. I am what I've made of myself. With the help of others. The kind of help I hope I can give your niece, my lord." She paused, then pushed for the close. "Do we have a deal?"

He regarded her silently and speculatively for several long moments. Rebel held her breath. She had no more tactics to play. She had used up all her weapons. All she could do now was will him to give in.

Very slowly his mouth curved into a smile. "Yes. I am interested in dealing with you for a week, Miss James. Having you as my guest here for that length of time should be quite decisive . . . one way or another."

Rebel's initial surge of relief was cut short by the strangest impression that he was not thinking of his niece at all. Her heart gave an odd flutter. He really was an extremely complex man, difficult to read and all the more intriguing and challenging because of it. But she had won the first foothold.

While she was contemplating her next move, a knock on the door heralded the arrival of afternoon tea. A tall, rather spindly man attired in formal dress entered, pushing a tea-trolley with an air of great dignity. His sparse hair was white, and although his cheeks had a ruddy glow and his skin was relatively unwrinkled, Rebel placed his age at close to seventy.

"I thought Mrs. Tomkins told me you were unwell, Brooks," Lord Davenport remarked in surprise.

"A slight indisposition," came the somewhat pained reply. "I'm quite able to look after your guests, m'lord."

Clearly this was a matter of pride. Or curiosity. He cast a measuring look at Rebel, checking out the report that the housekeeper had undoubtedly given him.

"My butler," Lord Davenport informed Rebel by way of introduction. "Miss James will be my guest here over this coming week, Brooks."

"I'm sure all the staff will make you welcome, Miss James," Brooks said with authority.

Rebel smiled at him. "Thank you."

He made an elegant ceremony of serving afternoon tea, and again Rebel was forcibly reminded of the refined niceties of this world that the Earl of Stanthorpe occupied. The silver tea-service, the fine china, the delicate little sandwiches, scones and clotted cream and homemade strawberry jam, all laid on in a graceful style that was completely taken for granted.

It could become very seductive, Rebel realised, yet it had no relevance at all to what counted most in the hearts and minds of people. Lord Davenport did not have the aura of a contented man, and although the circumstances were vastly different, his niece was every bit as much of a lost child as Rebel herself had been.

This latter thought recollected her original purpose for coming to Davenport Hall. She eyed the butler speculatively as he made a dignified withdrawal. A week gave her ample opportunity to ask everyone on the estate about the war orphans who had stayed here, and Brooks was surely old enough to remember that time.

"Has your butler been with your family very long, Lord Davenport?" she asked the moment they were alone again.

"Since the war."

"Not during?"

"He served in the army. Most able-bodied young men did." A wry smile tilted his mouth. "Brooks really should be retired but he would be mortally wounded if I insisted on his giving up his position here. Some days he is slightly indisposed. A weakness for a glass of port, I'm afraid, but I don't begrudge him a little self-indulgence. Mrs. Tomkins fills in for him when needs must.''

So Brooks couldn't tell her anything about her mother, Rebel thought with a little stab of disappointment. But surely there would be someone who knew someone who might remember. It was only a question of asking at a suitable moment. Which wasn't now. Rebel dragged her mind off that train of thought and concentrated on the more important issue of Celeste.

It struck her as very telling that Lord Davenport had spoken of his butler with warm indulgence, yet both warmth and indulgence were withheld from his niece. Not once had he spoken of her with even a trace of affection. But obviously he was capable of affection. He wasn't made entirely of ice.

She looked up to find him watching her, and the expression in his eyes was definitely not that of a man of ice. There was no aristocratic blue blood about it at all, but pure red-blooded male interest, and it instantly sent a surge of heat through Rebel's veins.

''You haven't told me your full name, Miss James,'' he said with an inviting smile. ''Since you're to be my guest, it would be a more convincing scenario for Celeste if we moved onto a less formal mode of address, don't you think? My guests would normally call me Hugh.''

Rebel took a deep breath. When he chose to exert charm, Hugh Davenport was almost lethally attractive. He certainly had a most unsettling effect on her. All her nerves seemed to be tingling.

"Thank you. It is best, but I didn't want to presume too much," she replied. "My full name is Rebel Griffith James."

"Rebel." His mouth twitched with that secret inner amusement. "An unusual name. I'll have no problem remembering it. When should we expect you tomorrow?"

"If you could have a car call for me at ten o'clock in the morning, I'll be ready to leave by then."

"Your address in Mayfair?" he asked, reaching into an inner coat pocket and drawing out a gold pen and a slim notebook.

She gave it to him and he wrote it down.

"I'll tell Celeste you'll be here by lunchtime," he said dryly as he put the pen and notebook away.

"Thank you." Since he had reopened the subject of his niece, Rebel quickly pressed it further. "It would be helpful if you'd give me some background knowledge on your niece before I meet her again. She told me that both her parents were dead. If you wouldn't mind outlining the circumstances..."

His face tightened.

Rebel paused, instantly aware that she had entered sensitive ground again. The ice man was back, and she steeled herself to fend off a rebuke.

"My brother died on a skiing slope in Switzerland," came the cold reply. "I inherited his title, and Celeste, six months ago."

The edge of bitterness in his voice warned Rebel of complexities that could have a lot of bearing on Celeste's behaviour. "I'm sorry," she said quietly. "I didn't realise that her father was the earl before you. And that the bereavement was so recent."

It was a possible explanation for why there was no bonding between uncle and niece. Sometimes grief drew people together, but obviously not in this case. In fact, Celeste had displayed no grief whatsoever at the loss of her parents. Although that could be a defensive reaction.

"When did her mother die?" Rebel asked softly, needing to know in order to gain a better understanding of the little girl.

"On the day of my brother's funeral. An accident on the motorway to London."

This was delivered in a tone that suggested a grim satisfaction in the timing of his sister-in-law's death. She searched the dark eyes for some clue to his feelings, but they revealed nothing. Their darkness was so total it was spine-chilling.

"That must have been very harrowing," she said sympathetically.

There was a flash of something savage in his eyes—malevolent triumph?—but it was so quickly erased that Rebel wasn't sure she hadn't imagined it.

"The last six months have not been easy," he answered flatly.

"Was Celeste in the car with her mother?" Rebel asked, wondering if the accident had traumatised the child.

"No. Christine left her here. Celeste has been in my care since then." His mouth twisted. "Whether you believe it or not, I have done the best I can for her."

Rebel discreetly refrained from any comment on that score. He might have done his best by his lights, but he had a lot to learn about children, in her opinion.

"Celeste said you go away and leave her alone here," she put forward testingly.

"Hardly alone," he mocked. "It's true my work takes me away. I do have responsibilities to other people besides my niece. I'm not just an idle earl, living off my heritage. In fact, I did not anticipate being an earl at all. I'm in the wine trade. Which necessitates regular visits to the vineyards in France and Germany."

"I see," she murmured, accepting that he did have reason for his absences, but thinking that he might have delegated such trips to someone else—at least some of them—given his new responsibilities to a child. "You didn't think Celeste needed more of your time throughout this period of change?" she asked softly.

He sighed. Wearily. "Celeste's pattern of behaviour was set long before she came into my care. *I* did not turn her into a monster. And before you protest that description, it was the term used by the nanny I rescued from the gazebo. She informed me—in a state of near hysteria—that the child needed locking up and the key thrown away. I might add that every nanny Celeste has ever had, from the time she was little more than an infant, has expressed a similar view. Nothing has changed. And that is a matter of record, not just my word."

"Locking the child up and throwing away the key is not a solution," Rebel stated with passionate conviction.

"It does provide some temporary peace for those whose lives she makes miserable," he returned pointedly. "Which includes everyone in this household. But I do agree, it is not a solution. I freely confess I have no solution. However, since *you* believe you can redeem the child, I certainly won't stand in the way of that possibility."

His disbelief was patent.

He did not expect her to achieve anything with Celeste.

"I shall be most interested in watching your progress with her this week," he added, but Rebel felt they were only glib words.

"Interested enough, I hope, to cooperate with me in whatever I think is necessary for your niece's welfare," she pressed.

"If you think toe crushing is in order, I won't interfere," he assured her, the dark eyes lightly mocking her methods. "You have a free hand in dealing with Celeste however you see fit."

"Thank you. Are you also willing to be more than a passive watcher?"

He frowned. "What are you asking, Rebel?"

"If you will act on my advice."

"That would depend entirely on the advice. Acting is not one of my talents. There would be no point in my trying to do something against my convictions."

"Fair enough," Rebel conceded. "Will you make time this week to be here as much as possible?"

He laughed, a low chuckle that seemed to pummel Rebel's stomach. The dark eyes danced at her in amused challenge. A man-woman challenge. "Yes, I will certainly make time to be at hand all week. The experience you offer is quite enough to draw me away from work."

Rebel's heart slammed against her chest as the realisation hit home. Hugh Davenport was taking her as a guest for one purpose only, and that purpose had nothing whatsoever to do with his niece. He felt the same attraction she felt, and now that he was assured that she wasn't some form of con woman, he wanted to explore it further.

Rebel was suddenly confused by a mixture of apprehension and excitement. She also wanted to explore her feelings towards this man further, yet she couldn't let that get in the way of helping Celeste. On the other hand, perhaps Hugh Davenport's desire for her company could be turned to advantage where Celeste was concerned. Although that would certainly be a very tricky game to play.

All's fair in love and war, Rebel recited to herself. The child needed to be loved, and Rebel decided that if she had to war with both herself and Hugh Davenport to gain that end, any means was justified.

Having sorted herself out to her satisfaction, Rebel smiled at Hugh Davenport and rose to her feet. "I must be going. I have a lot to do before tomorrow."

"Of course."

A ripple of awareness coursed through Rebel's body as he stood up and smiled at her. Her first instincts were right, she thought. She was wading into deep and dangerous waters with this man.

"Since you don't have a car. . ."

"I came by motor scooter. It's parked near the gateway."

His eyes flicked down her black leather outfit, making her temperature rise. "I see," he murmured, his mouth curling with irony. "In that case, I'll escort you out."

He walked beside her, courteously opening doors for her but not saying another word until they were on the portico.

"I think I must owe you several apologies," he remarked as they headed for the steps.

Rebel laughed and shook her head. "I think, perhaps, I owe you one or two myself. Let's call it quits."

He slanted her an amused look. "If that's another deal, I'll take it."

She gave him an impish smile. "Agreed."

He chuckled to himself, and Rebel's heart performed aerobics all the way down the steps and around the circular fountain. It was madness to feel like this, she chided herself. Mad to fall into flirting with this hopelessly unsuitable attraction in any way whatsoever. Where could it lead? Only to an emotional mess, that's where! Titles might not mean anything to her, but the English were renowned for holding to their class system. She very much doubted that the Earl of Stanthorpe would be any different in that respect.

An experience. That's all he wanted with her.

He had said it straight out.

"What brought you to Davenport Hall, Rebel?" he asked as they started up the long avenue.

She glanced at the vast spread of branches overhead, like a beautiful canopy with the delicate intertwining of pretty green leaves. Once again she had the eerie sensation of walking down a tunnel of timelessness. Was her mother watching from somewhere? A little girl, orphaned as Rebel herself had been, as Celeste was.

"Perhaps it was fate," she answered, still bemused by her thoughts. She felt his sharp look and turned her head to meet it.

"I don't believe in fate," he said flatly.

Rebel decided this was as good a time as any to tell him the truth. "I wanted to see Davenport Hall. My mother was a war orphan, and for six months before she was shipped to Australia, she was sheltered here. Along with forty or so other orphans."

"Shipped to Australia?" he questioned with a frown that suggested such an idea was barely acceptable.

"It *was* done, Hugh," Rebel assured him. "My mother was only five years old at the time. But she never forgot this place. I only meant to have a look at it, but when I got to the gateway, I wanted to see more. So I parked my motor scooter, walked up this avenue and rang the bell at the front door, meaning to ask permission to look around."

"Just like that," he said dryly.

"I was expecting to have to sell the idea."

"No doubt you would have done it," he remarked even more dryly.

There was no need, Rebel thought with satisfaction. She had a whole week to find out a lot of things—about her mother, Celeste, the man beside her. And if she managed as well as she hoped to, a week could stretch into longer period of time. Who knew how long?

They reached the end of the avenue and Rebel diverted from the driveway to push her motor scooter out from its resting place by the stone wall. Hugh Davenport waited, watching her with a dark brooding intensity that made Rebel's skin prickle. He did not speak again until she was seated on the scooter and preparing to put on her safety helmet.

"Do you really believe you can work some miracle with Celeste?" he suddenly asked.

"Yes," she answered seriously. "I wouldn't have fought you over it if I didn't think I could do some good, Hugh. Perhaps not a miracle in so short a time. But I do know that the challenge I offer her will have an effect."

"Don't count on too much, Rebel." It was spoken in a soft, kindly tone. "Others as well-meaning as you have tried and failed. Celeste . . ." His mouth twisted in distaste. "Celeste is Christine's daughter. That is inescapable."

He gave her a grim smile. "Until tomorrow."

Then he swung on his heel and strode off down the tunnel of timelessness, leaving Rebel to wonder if she should ever have stepped off the motor scooter.

There was a darkness here. A darkness that could very well swallow her up and tear her apart. The child so disturbed. The man with hatred eating at his heart, hatred for the child and the child's mother. Somehow Rebel had little doubt about that now. Yet even as she recognised the dangers in committing herself to doing something about it, she was conscious of a fascination she couldn't deny.

CHAPTER FOUR

IT WAS ALMOST NOON when Rebel entered the gateway to Davenport Hall the next day. As the chauffeured Rolls-Royce purred slowly up the avenue, Rebel tried once more to quell all the misgivings that had plagued her since she had left here yesterday. Normally she was absolutely clear-minded about any decision she made. The difference this time was the high degree of her emotional involvement with the people she would be dealing with.

Perhaps she identified too closely with the child. It could lead her badly astray with Celeste, whose problems might be far more complex than Rebel had anticipated. As for the man, it was difficult for Rebel to comprehend why she reacted to him the way she did. She was not in the habit of losing her head in any situation, yet he stirred responses in her that seemed to have a will of their own. It complicated everything.

The car rounded the stone fountain and came to a smooth halt at the foot of the steps. Rebel looked up at the formidable front doors of a huge mansion, distinctly uneasy about what lay in store for her behind them. One of them opened and out flew a little figure in blue. Rebel's heart instantly lifted. No matter where it led or what pitfalls she would meet, her decision had been right. This lost little girl needed her.

By the time the chauffeur opened Rebel's door, Celeste was halfway down the steps. "You did come!" she cried, pulling to a surprised halt as Rebel stepped out of the car. The angelic face was stamped with incredulity.

"I sure did," Rebel replied with an encouraging grin, even while ruefully wondering what Celeste had planned for the visitor if it had been someone else. Clearly she had mistrusted whatever her uncle had told her.

"Are you really going to stay?" Celeste demanded suspiciously.

"Why not? This is a nice place. I'm going to enjoy staying here. I'm glad your uncle invited me."

The big blue eyes flicked past Rebel to where the chauffeur was lifting bags out of the car. Reassured by this evidence, she eyed Rebel up and down, taking in the Reeboks on her feet, the figure-hugging blue jeans and the brightly patterned jumper that depicted a whole lot of Australian motifs.

The outfit was not a far cry from what she had worn yesterday, and Rebel had deliberately chosen it, aware that a change of image would unsettle the impression she had already made on the little girl. The satisfied look on Celeste's face rewarded the forethought.

"Was I supposed to dress up?" Rebel asked, eyeing Celeste's dress in return appraisal. The pintucking and rows of lace on the blue voile placed it in designer class.

Celeste shook her head. "I had to go to church," she explained. "This is a church dress. But you don't have to go to church, Rebel. That was this morning." Satisfied that she had got that issue out of the way, she pointed to the little white animals knitted into Rebel's jumper. "Are those sheep?"

"Yes. This is my Waltzing Matilda jumper. It pictures the story of the song."

"What story?" Celeste demanded, eagerly taking the bait.

As they walked up the steps together, Rebel told her the old Australian legend of the swagman who had stolen a lamb to eat. Then when he was caught by the troopers, he drowned himself in a billabong rather than be taken to jail.

Brooks was at the door to greet her and welcome her to Davenport Hall. The old butler looked surprised that Celeste was tagging along quite happily with Rebel. Mrs. Tomkins was waiting in the hallway to show Rebel to her room, and she also darted surprised glances at the little girl who accompanied them, peppering the new visitor with questions about swagmen and billabongs—foreign words to her, which had to be explained at great length.

Rebel was ushered into a fine room on the first floor, the finest she had ever been offered or occupied. It was a suite, one half taken up with a magnificent four-poster bed and attendant furniture, all valuable antiques, fulfilling their destiny for each honoured occupant for the past hundred years.

The other half was fitted out like a sitting room, with armchairs grouped around a fireplace, table and chairs, a writing desk, a television set and a bookcase filled with a wide range of novels. The thick carpet was a dusky pink and the furnishings were a mixture of rose-patterned chintz and cream silk. An adjoining dressing room, which was lined with roomy cupboards, led to a luxuriously appointed bathroom.

Rebel concluded guests at Davenport Hall were provided with every comfort and convenience money could buy. Certainly she was being given the red carpet treatment as far as her accommodation was concerned.

Her bags were brought up for her. Mrs. Tomkins offered her a maid to do the unpacking and any ironing that might be required. Rebel declined this offer, preferring to unpack her own things, which were mostly of uncrushable fabrics for easy travelling. Apart from which, the distraction of a maid bustling around would hinder the rapport she was forming with Celeste.

"Lunch is at one o'clock," Mrs. Tomkins informed her as she prepared to take her leave. "When you're ready, Miss James, Lord Davenport asked that you join him and his other guests in the drawing room."

This was said with a slight emphasis on "other guests." A glance at Rebel's casual outfit was hint enough that Mrs. Tomkins found Rebel's choice of clothes as doubtful in taste as the earl had done yesterday. While Rebel did espouse the principle of when in Rome, do as the Romans do, impressing the Earl of Stanthorpe's other guests was not her aim. In fact, she suspected that if she were to change her clothes, Celeste might interpret the action in a negative fashion.

"Thank you, Mrs. Tomkins," Rebel said with an appreciative smile. "We'll be down soon."

As soon as the housekeeper had departed Rebel tossed Celeste a leading question to make sure she was on the right track with the little girl. "Do you know who your uncle's other visitors are?"

"'Course I do," came the truculent reply. She eyed Rebel with simmering suspicion, a mutinous set to her mouth.

Rebel continued hanging up her dresses, pretending not to notice the change of expression. "Do you like them?" she asked offhandedly.

"I hate them!" Celeste burst out vehemently.

Which settled the question of clothes. If she dressed like them, Celeste would undoubtedly retreat from her. Besides, what she had on was perfectly respectable in the ordinary world. "Fine feathers might make fine birds, but clothes do not maketh the man," Rebel recited to herself, thereby quelling the treacherous desire for Hugh Davenport's approval.

Rebel directed a puzzled frown at Celeste. "You seem to do a lot of hating, kid. Which isn't a really smart thing. Have you got a reason for hating these people?"

Celeste frowned, calculating out how to reject the notion that she wasn't smart. "I've got reasons," she said triumphantly. "Sir Roger always laughs at me. And Lady Harriet says stupid things. And Cynthia Lumleigh is snaky."

"Snaky?" Rebel quizzed.

Celeste nodded knowingly. "You'll see."

"Okay. I'll wait and see," Rebel agreed, aware that children could be a lot more perceptive than adults gave them credit for. "How old are you?"

"I'm seven."

"And this Cynthia Lumleigh, is she your age?"

"No. She's grown up." The perfect little nose wrinkled in disgust. "She's after Uncle Hugh. She thinks she's so smart. I hate her worse than the others."

Which probably meant that Cynthia Lumleigh threatened what little sense of security Celeste had. The idea of Cynthia did not appeal to Rebel, either. But seeing Hugh Davenport with another woman— one of his own kind—would probably help to get her feet firmly on the ground where he was concerned.

Rebel smiled. "Well, I guess I'll soon find out how smart she is for myself."

She excused herself to use the bathroom, quickly checking that her hair was as tidy as her long, unruly curls ever allowed it to be and that her lipstick needed no touching up. A glance at the full-length mirror in the dressing room assured her that at least she looked smart casual, not sloppy casual. She held out her hand to Celeste as she entered the bedroom and gave the little girl an encouraging grin.

"Come on. Time to put our best foot forward and fight the good fight. The trick is not to let anyone get to you."

Celeste looked uncertainly at Rebel's hand, then decided she would take a chance with it. "How do you do that?" she demanded.

Rebel was careful only to hold the child's hand lightly as they set off for the drawing room. "The first thing you do is try to work out what is really happening," she explained. "Like Sir Roger, for example. I don't know about him yet, but a lot of people laugh when they're not sure of what to say or do. A laugh covers things up for them when they're really feeling uncertain inside. It needn't mean that they find something funny at all."

"You mean they're, not smart," Celeste commented thoughtfully.

"That's right. You sure catch on fast," Rebel said admiringly. "But it's not kind to point it out to them because they're already feeling not sure what to do, and that makes them feel worse. So you smile to make them feel better. That way you win, because then they think you're a nice person, and you feel good because you've made them feel good. The same thing goes for people who say silly things. They don't really want to say silly things. Most of the time they just don't know what to say, so they say anything that comes into their heads."

"Do you smile at them, too?" Celeste queried.

Rebel grinned at her. "Sure do. That makes them feel good, and you win again."

"What about snaky people?"

"Smiles are still good, because then they can't see if they've hurt you or not. Snaky people like to see that they've hurt you, so you beat them by not showing it. A smile makes them think they've lost."

"But they do hurt," Celeste argued.

"Yes. Sometimes they do. Sometimes you've got to fight back. But picking the right time for that is very tricky. Sometimes it's best to wait a while, and then you deliver a king hit."

"A king hit?" Celeste looked fascinated.

They had reached the doors to the drawing room. "I'll tell you about that another time," Rebel promised her. "We'd better get our smiles into gear. How's this?" Rebel tried out her best toothpaste advertisement.

Celeste giggled and nodded approval.

"Now you," Rebel demanded.

The little girl showed a perfect row of teeth.

"Fine!" Rebel approved, inwardly exulting that Celeste was proving so responsive. "In we go, smiles at the ready."

Their entrance into the drawing room instantly drew the eyes of all those present. As conversation lapsed and silence fell, Rebel felt Celeste's fingers tighten around hers, as though claiming possession. She turned a light squeeze of reassurance as her gaze flicked past the company and fastened on Hugh Davenport. He stood in front of the fireplace, the commanding position a natural focus, but he compelled all her attention anyway, the dark riveting eyes locking onto hers and seeming to bore into her soul.

He wore a three-piece suit, dark blue-black with a classic pinstripe. A red and silver-grey tie set off the pristine whiteness of his shirt. The clothes emphasised his dark good looks in a stunning fashion, and Rebel was all too aware of her heart beating a quick protest within her suddenly constricted chest.

His gaze dropped abruptly, drawn by the apparently unbelievable sight of Celeste's hand linked to hers. His eyebrows drew together as his gaze moved to Rebel's jeans and up to her face again. The dark eyes seared hers with questions. Rebel determinedly ignored the wild pitter-pattering of her heart and added a few watts to her smile. It drew an answering curve of ironic appreciation from him.

"A pleasure to have you with us again, Rebel," he said smoothly. One eyebrow lifted sardonically as he added, "I trust Celeste has made you welcome?"

"Very much so," Rebel returned, with a conspiratorial grin at the little girl.

Celeste turned a smug grin up to her uncle. "Now I know all about Waltzing Matilda," she told him. "The story is knitted into Rebel's jumper."

All eyes fastened on Rebel's chest.

"How novel!" A sweetly indulgent remark from the svelte blonde whom Rebel immediately identified as Cynthia Lumleigh.

"Very becoming!" Sir Roger said, then gave an embarrassed laugh as he realised his gaze had lingered on Rebel's breasts.

"They do the cleverest things these days," Lady Harriet gushed.

"I see," Hugh Davenport murmured, his dark eyes knowingly mocking Rebel's tactic. *It won't last,* they told her.

Don't bet on it, Rebel beamed back at him, adrenalin running high. Somehow he stoked a fire in her that she couldn't dampen, however much she told herself to stay cool.

The silent interchange did not go unnoticed by Cynthia Lumleigh, who gave a tinkling laugh to draw attention to herself. "We're embarrassing your guest, Hugh. Aren't you going to introduce us?"

"I doubt very much that anything could embarrass Rebel," he said dryly. "I've never met anyone who takes so much in her stride."

His eyes twinkled an amused challenge as he moved to draw her into the group. "You aren't embarrassed, are you?"

"Not in the least," she answered lightly.

The twinkle left his eyes as he looked at his niece. "I hope you remember what I said, Celeste."

"Yes, Uncle Hugh," came the resentful reply.

Undoubtedly she had been given a harsh warning to behave, Rebel thought. She gave Celeste's hand a friendly squeeze. The little girl lifted a sulky face. Rebel flashed her the toothpaste smile. It took a moment to register, but the perfect row of teeth was finally bared. Rebel gave her hand an approving squeeze. The little hand squeezed back in conspiratorial agreement.

Hugh Davenport was obviously perplexed by this strange byplay. He frowned at both of them. He got two fixed smiles in return. He shrugged and moved smoothly into performing introductions.

Lady Harriet was definitely a gusher. "So interesting to meet you... And the balloon race. Hugh was just telling us about it. And you all the way from Australia. So far to come."

"Down Under, they call it, my dear," Sir Roger boomed, then laughed as he grasped Rebel's hand.

Rebel gave him an extra big smile in case Celeste was watching.

There was no harm in either of them. Rebel sensed that immediately. They looked to be both in their forties, a comfortable couple with no pretensions of greatness about them. The church clothes were well-tailored country tweeds, although the pearl and ruby brooch on the lapel of Lady Harriet's suit coat was clearly real.

Cynthia Lumleigh was their niece, and she was an entirely different kettle of fish. She could have been a clone of Princess Di, her tall, slim figure elegantly attired in a white silk suit, her blonde hair artfully arranged in a soft fly-away style, her blue eyes subtly emphasised with clever make-up. But her charm was suspect from the start. No sooner had they all sat down, Rebel and Celeste on one sofa, Sir Roger and Lady Harriet facing them, Cynthia and Hugh in paired armchairs, than the sly digs started.

"Griffith-James sounds familiar," Cynthia mused with sweet condescension. "Should I know the name?"

"Since we've never met before, I shouldn't think so," Rebel answered dryly. "Griffith was my mother's name. James is my surname. They're not hyphenated."

"Oh! It sounded so distinctive." The condescension took on an extra twist as Cynthia added, "Not at all colonial."

Celeste was spot on, Rebel thought. Definitely snaky. Rebel smiled pure syrup. "I'm afraid you're behind the times, Miss Lumleigh. Australia stopped being a British colony almost a hundred years ago."

Out of the corner of her eye Rebel saw Hugh's lips twitch.

Cynthia tinkled a laugh. "Of course. But you still consider England the mother country, don't you?"

If the question had been put in a less patronising manner, Rebel would probably have answered yes. There were emotional and traditional ties to Britain. But she was not about to be established as some kind of second-class citizen, not in anyone's mind. If Cynthia Lumleigh wanted to prove herself superior, she would have to do it on her own merits, not on some nationality basis.

"Have you ever been to Australia, Miss Lumleigh?" Rebel asked.

"Good heavens, no!" Cynthia's shrug was derisively dismissive. "It is rather the end of the earth."

"That's one point of view," Rebel replied, matching the tone of derisive dismissal, but sweetening it with a broad smile. "Some people might consider Australia the beginning of the earth. It is, after all, a far more ancient land than Britain. And it has a way of stamping its own unique impact on people. I think you would find it bears very little relationship to England. Apart from a few sports and our system of government."

"Yes. There's that," Hugh chimed in, his eyes dancing appreciation of Rebel's argument. "But for the rest..." He turned to the blonde. "If you ever go, don't expect a little England, Cynthia. It really is a foreign country."

"*You've* been there, Hugh?"

Having found no joy in trying to put Rebel down, Cynthia concentrated all her attention on holding her host's attention, asking endless questions about his trip to Australia where he had been invited to judge wines. Rebel felt a rush of warm pleasure when Hugh acknowledged that some Australian wines were amongst the finest he'd ever tasted. Certainly his complimentary remarks about her country more than made up for his girlfriend's snide cracks.

Cynthia, however, was not interested in a topic that Rebel could share. She started raving on about her last trip to France, making sure Rebel was excluded from the conversation and keeping Hugh focused on herself.

She was very good at it. But while her target responded as demanded, Rebel grew more and more sure that Hugh Davenport's affections were not engaged with Cynthia Lumleigh. He was polite. He was charming. He might even take her as a suitable wife. But he was not in love with the snaky blonde. Rebel knew what that looked like. Her brother-in-law was very much in love with his wife, Rebel's sister Tiffany. It showed.

Not that it was any of her business, Rebel told herself. Except, of course, it would be a disaster for Celeste to come under Cynthia Lumleigh's thumb. Rebel hoped that Hugh Davenport had enough sense to see that.

Brooks came in to announce lunch. He led the way to a light and bright informal dining room. The furniture was white and modern, which surprised Rebel, but there was an elegance about it that was enhanced by the sheer spaciousness of the room. The long windows overlooked a rose garden, and the deep yellow of the curtains was repeated on the chair cushions. Yellow linen serviettes set in silver holders added splashes of colour to the white cloth on the oval table, and a low bowl of yellow rosebuds made a delightful centrepiece.

The host moved naturally to the far end of the table. Cynthia Lumleigh was placed at Hugh's right hand, Lady Harriet on his left. Rebel was to be seated next to Cynthia and opposite Sir Roger, with Celeste between them facing her uncle, but Cynthia suddenly decided to interfere with this arrangement.

"Celeste, my dear, come and sit by me," she invited, her smile at the little girl a new high in sickening indulgence. "You've been such a good girl today. A real little angel."

She held out her hand, obviously intent on testing the child's allegiance to Rebel—or stirring a scene that would end with both Rebel and Celeste the losers. Rebel squeezed Celeste's hand hard. The child looked at her with sheer mutiny in her eyes. Rebel outdid her toothpaste smile.

"Sir Roger will have to miss out on having you beside him, Celeste, but I'll still have the pleasure of having you next to me," she said pointedly.

Sir Roger laughed.

Celeste bared her teeth at him, then having got in some practice, she turned even more teeth on Cynthia. However, she steadfastly ignored the outstretched hand as she changed places with Rebel.

Cynthia heaved a disappointed sigh and looked at Hugh as if to say she had tried but the child was impossible.

Hugh did not return the look.

His lips were twitching.

He didn't shoot a challenge at Rebel, either.

He turned to Lady Harriet and engaged her in conversation about a fete she was organising. Rebel gathered that the village church was in need of repair and that Lady Harriet headed a committee in charge of raising the necessary funds. The discussion of what could be done continued throughout the first course of vegetable soup and the main meal of roast beef. Rebel didn't mind not taking part in the exchange of ideas on fund-raising. Every so often, when Sir Roger laughed, she exchanged smiles with Celeste, making a secret game of it, which kept the little girl interested and amused.

The private byplay did not escape Hugh Davenport's notice. Occasionally he threw a dark, penetrating look at Rebel, probing for what she was up to. This did not escape Cynthia Lumleigh's notice. Piqued by these silent interchanges that suggested an intimacy she found threatening, she turned her sweet brand of venom on Rebel once again.

"I'm sure you must have some interesting ideas for the fete, Miss James. Your charity work with the balloon race suggests you've had loads of experience."

Rebel shot a hard, probing look at Hugh Davenport, wondering if he had deliberately misled his guests about what she was doing in England so that they would find her presence here more acceptable. Rebel scorned the kind of snobbery that looked down at working-class people. Pride in her own self-worth insisted on a correction.

"You must have misunderstood whatever Lord Davenport told you, Miss Lumleigh." She produced an indulgently forgiving smile. "While the race itself will benefit a charity, my work on it is strictly business. I was contracted to sell the sponsorships, and I'll be earning a considerable fee for delivering the agreed number."

Cynthia raised her eyebrows. "Oh, I see," she drawled. "Then you're a career girl, Miss James."

Rebel grinned at her as she shot down the implications raised by the blonde's snaky tone of voice. "If you mean I enjoy the career I've made for myself, yes. If you mean I'm dedicated to it for life, no. I'd like nothing more than to marry someone I love and raise a very large family."

Cynthia didn't care for that answer at all.

But Hugh Davenport's lips twitched.

The blonde tried another attack. "With the population problems we have in the world today, having a large family doesn't show much social consciousness, Miss James," she said in sweet-mannered reproof.

Rebel gave a soft little laugh. "Miss Lumleigh, I've been brought up in a very large family with more social conscience than probably any other family in the world. In fact, you could call it a family of nations, since so many of my brothers and sisters come from different countries."

That bamboozled Cynthia.

Lady Harriet, however, was intrigued. "What do you mean?" she asked.

Rebel smiled at her, conscious that Hugh Davenport's interest was also captured. Rebel hoped he would take the point that her life experience really did equip her with a special knowledge of how to handle traumatised children.

"All fourteen of us were adopted, Lady Harriet. Zachary Lee came from America, Tiffany Makana from Fiji, Carol and Alan Tay from Vietnam, Zuang Chi from China, Mahammad and Leah from India, Rosalie from the Philippines, Kim from Korea, Shasti from Ethiopia, Suzanne from Canada, Joseph from Thailand and Tom is a native Australian."

The list brought a dumbfounded silence.

Rebel looked at Hugh Davenport. He stared at her, his expression one of high-intensity appraisal. Rebel felt a glow of triumphant satisfaction. That would teach him he shouldn't make generalisations about people, she thought.

"What about you?" Lady Harriet asked. "Where do you come from?"

Rebel had to drag her mind off the nerve-tingling sense of contest that Hugh Davenport inspired. "I was born in Australia, but I'm always referred to as the English one within the family. My mother was English, and when the James family adopted me, I had a very English accent."

"Remarkable!" Sir Roger said. And laughed.

"However did your parents handle such a mix?" Lady Harriet asked, shaking her head in amazement.

Rebel's eyes bored into the dark ones facing her, determined to punch the point home. "With love. And a great deal of cherishing," she said slowly.

But you've got to earn respect first, she added silently. And show that you care!

Cynthia Lumleigh, however, was not about to sit by and allow Rebel to be an authority on anything. "What happened to your real parents, Miss James?" she asked with arch interest. Her eyes glinted with the need to score off Rebel, and with unerring aim she was zeroing in on the obviously vulnerable ground.

"I lost them," Rebel answered evenly. "We all lost our real parents before we were adopted."

"But you must remember your mother," came the silky reminder. "Since you learnt your English accent from her."

"She died when I was five," Rebel answered briefly, knowing what was coming next but not know how to evade it.

"And your father?"

Rebel dredged up a smile. "I never knew him."

"How sad!" Cynthia dripped acid sympathy. "Did he die before you were born?"

Rebel looked her straight in the eye, but somehow she just couldn't hold her smile. "No. He deserted my mother before I was born. I have no idea whether my natural father is dead or alive. Nor do I know who or what he was. Or is." Even now she felt the temptation to add, "And I don't care! He means nothing to me!" But she knew how defensive and untrue that statement was. Of course she cared. It would be unnatural not to care and feel rejected by the sense of desertion. That was a problem one had to live with.

Cynthia gloated. Having established Rebel's lack of respectable lineage, she was all the more smug in her superiority. "How distressing for you!" she dripped, savouring her triumph.

Rebel was about to say that her adoptive father had more than filled that hole in her life when Celeste intervened.

The little girl reached out and knocked her glass of water, sending it flying into Cynthia's lap. As a king hit it was certainly effective. But the time was extremely ill-chosen. It was not a winning move.

"Oh! You wicked child! You did that deliberately!" the blonde screeched, leaping up from her chair and wailing in distress at the despoiling of her silk suit.

Hugh Davenport instantly rose to his feet, his face tightening, his lips thinning, his eyes shooting ice daggers at his niece.

Celeste glared in rebellious defiance.

There was only one way to avoid a damaging scene.

Rebel scrambled up from her chair, orchestrating an agitated gesture that knocked her glass of red wine across the table and into Celeste's lap. "Oh, heavens! Look what I've done now!" she cried, distracting Hugh Davenport from the rebuke that was obviously about to break from his lips.

Rebel swooped on Celeste, lifting her out of the chair and hoisting her up in her arms. "What a mess we've made over everything with our clumsiness!" she gabbled in eloquent dismay, clutching Celeste tightly to her. "Please excuse us, everyone. I'll take Celeste to her room for a change of clothes. The wine will stain if it's not washed out straight away. So lucky you only got watered, Miss Lumleigh."

She hurried to the doorway before Celeste recovered from the shock tactics and spoiled the whole show with a defiant tantrum. Rebel paused just long enough to throw a look of apologetic appeal at the disarrayed company. They were all staring after her, Cynthia Lumleigh with venom, Sir Roger and Lady Harriet with their mouths agape, Hugh Davenport with a hard, mocking challenge in his dark eyes.

Rebel tried for a last diplomatic touch. "I'm terribly sorry about the tablecloth, Hugh. Lady Harriet, I do hope the church fete is a great success. Sir Roger, Miss Lumleigh, it was lovely meeting you all. Perhaps we'll meet again some other time."

It was as good an exit line as any, and before anyone found wits enough to respond, Rebel was off, carrying Celeste out of the crisis centre. It might be cowardly to run away, Rebel thought ruefully, but at least you lived to fight another day.

CHAPTER FIVE

IT WAS NOT THE EASIEST of afternoons. Celeste considered her king hit on Cynthia Lumleigh entirely justified. She didn't care what Uncle Hugh said to her. She didn't care what anyone thought. Cynthia Lumleigh had been mean and snaky, and Rebel hadn't smiled back.

She was not at all convinced by Rebel's explanation that it was the memory of a bad time that had hurt, not Cynthia Lumleigh's snakiness. However, she did eventually agree to let Rebel fight her own fights from now on. But she still wasn't sorry about spilling the water. And since, in her heart of hearts, Rebel wasn't sorry about it, either, she let the subject drop.

A long walk around the estate seemed to be the best way of keeping out of trouble. The grounds were immaculately kept. Paths of paving stones led to various formal gardens laid out within well-clipped hedges. Beyond a perfect croquet lawn was an ornamental lake, and overlooking this was the infamous gazebo where Celeste had imprisoned the nanny. However, Rebel refrained from comment on that incident. It was Celeste's future that concerned her, not the past.

Curiosity about the James family eventually drew Celeste out of her sulks, and Rebel told her the stories about how each child had been adopted. There were long silences while Celeste brooded over these histories. Rebel did not try to pry into the little girl's thoughts. She hoped Celeste was realising that there were many children who were a lot worse off than she was. It was not until the child's bedtime that Rebel began to realise how little Celeste had been given.

Mrs. Tomkins directed them to the library for Celeste to say goodnight to her uncle.

Rebel found this room redolent of a past age, its walls lined with glass-fronted bookcases, its vast floor space furnished with three impressive desks and a number of huge, heavily studded leather chairs. There were map cases, an antique globe of the world as well as a more modern one, huge dictionaries on reading stands, collections of encyclopaedias. The atmosphere seemed to be one of nostalgia for a store of knowledge that should always be kept and cherished.

Hugh Davenport was seated at the central desk, apparently looking through a large leather-bound journal. When he glanced up and saw who entered, he rose slowly to his feet, his demeanour cold and stern.

"Did you have a pleasant walk around the grounds?" he asked Rebel with distant politeness.

Rebel felt a little chill run down her spine. "Yes, thank you," she returned just as politely.

His gaze dropped to his niece. "Don't think I didn't see what you did at the lunch table today, Celeste. Rebel chose to cover up for you, and because she is our guest, and she chose to do that, I'll give you one more chance. But let there be any more of such disgraceful behaviour and you'll have all your meals in the kitchen in future. Is that clear?"

"I don't care!" Celeste burst out defiantly.

The dark eyes glittered at Rebel, mocking her contention that she could change Celeste's behaviour for the better. They sliced back to his niece.

"Whether you care or not, Celeste, is totally irrelevant to the point in question. You either do as you're told, or take the consequences," he stated bitingly.

"Celeste has come to say goodnight, Hugh," Rebel said before the little girl dug herself an even deeper grave with her uncle. Not that his attitude encouraged anything else, but now was not the time to tackle that. She squeezed Celeste's hand. "Say goodnight, Celeste."

There was a mutinous silence.

Hugh Davenport waited, his face as cold and stony as a statue, totally unhelpful. Rebel wanted to scream at him that his niece was only a little girl, not an enemy who had to be stared down.

Then, in a voice that quivered uncertainly, the words were finally pushed out. "Goodnight, Uncle Hugh."

He graciously nodded. "Goodnight, Celeste."

And that was it.

Dismissed without a grain of warmth, let alone a hug or a kiss!

Rebel worked hard at winning back the little girl's confidence. She tucked her into bed and told her a long, wild story about an Australian bushranger in the early colonial days. But there was no response in the big blue eyes. They stared at Rebel, passively waiting for her to finish and go. When she bent forward to kiss the child goodnight, Celeste shrank away from her, hiding her face in the pillow.

"Hey! Did I frighten you with that story?" Rebel asked.

The head jerked around. "'Course not! I just want to go to sleep now."

"Okay. But before you go to sleep we've got to have our hug and kiss."

"We haven't got to!" Celeste returned fiercely.

Rebel sighed. "I guess you're no good at it. Is that the problem, kid? You haven't had much practice at it?"

Silence. The little face had a tight, closed look.

"Hugging and kissing are like fighting," Rebel explained, determined to break through the barriers the child had erected. "If you want to be any good at all, you've got to practise them. At the end of every day we're going to forget any bad things that happen. To do that you've got to be hugged and kissed, or you just get to feeling terribly alone in the world and every bad thing seems worse. So you've got to learn how to do it really well, just as you've got to learn how to be a good fighter."

Rebel started sliding her hands under the child's shoulders. "If you put your arms around my neck, we can have a real good hug," she instructed softly.

There was a look of panic on the child's face, but she reached out tentatively and Rebel swept her up into an embrace before she could change her mind, rocking her in a tight hug as the little arms wound slowly around her neck and clung hard. The certainty flashed into Rebel's mind that Celeste had *never* been hugged and kissed goodnight, not by anyone! Yet surely that couldn't be right. Surely her mother or her father had shown her some affection.

Or had they?

Celeste had said she didn't care that they were dead. Would she have said that if they had ever shown her affection? Rebel decided she had a lot of talking to do with Hugh Davenport tonight. After she had settled Celeste in the way she should be settled.

"Mmm . . . you smell nice," she murmured approvingly, rubbing her face against the silky fair hair. Then very gently she laid the child down on the pillows, still holding her but easing away enough to smile at her. The blue eyes were huge. "Now I get to kiss you." She planted a soft kiss on the child's forehead. "And you get to kiss me."

"I can't reach your forehead," came the breathy whisper.

"How about my cheek? That will do fine."

The hands around Rebel's neck tightened as the child dived up to press her lips against Rebel's cheek. Then she dropped down, looking fearfully for criticism.

Rebel smiled. "You sure are a quick learner. Goodnight, Celeste."

It was the first time Rebel had used her name. There was a gleam of triumphant delight in the big blue eyes. Then, almost as if she was frightened that the feeling might be taken away, she quickly closed her eyes and snuggled her face into the pillow.

Rebel switched off the light and left the room, satisfied that she had made one giant step along the dif-

ficult road ahead, but there were a mighty lot of steps
to be still taken.

It was time to man battle stations!

When Celeste had been served her nursery tea, the
maid had informed Rebel that dinner was customar-
ily served at eight o'clock in the formal dining room.
It had only just gone seven. Rebel had plenty of time
to set up her strategy.

The right image was always important in her line of
work, and she had invested quite a bit of money in
good clothes. Since she was intent on softening up
Celeste's uncle, she chose the prettiest dress she had
brought with her. Half an hour later, having showered and changed, Rebel was well satisfied with her
appearance.

The silky fabric of her dress was brilliantly patterned in orange and yellow and designed in a soft
feminine style. The cape sleeves were double layered
and bordered with a band of yellow, as was the double frill on the swinging skirt and the biased frill highlighting the deep V neckline. The elasticised waist
emphasised the curvaciousness of her figure, and
Rebel was well aware that the dress flattered her colouring, picking up the gold speckles in her hazel eyes
and highlighting the dark, rich gleam of her luxuriant
brown curls. She added some generous dabs of Joy
perfume for good measure.

She found Hugh Davenport in the drawing room.
He was pouring himself some kind of drink from a
tray that held a number of crystal decanters and
glasses. He stopped in mid-action when he looked up
and saw her.

His eyes roved over the feminine fullness of her young body, seductively outlined by the softly clinging fabric. As she walked forward, the silky material shifted, sensuously moulding itself to the movement of her long legs, and his fascination with the effect held for several nerve-tingling seconds.

Eventually his good manners and breeding took over and his eyes dropped to the high-heeled yellow sandals strapped around her finely boned ankles before wrenching back up to her face.

"You look like the very essence of summer," he remarked softly. "Enough to gladden any eye."

It was a lovely compliment, enough to melt her resolution along with everything else. The way he had looked at her had made a total mess of her insides. But Rebel clung obstinately to her purpose.

"Thank you," she said. "I hope, if other guests should come by this evening, they'll think the same thing. I don't really care to be picked on as an inferior species twice in one day."

His mouth twitched. "Should anyone have that failure in judgment, I have no doubt that he or she will very shortly stand corrected. You have a definite gift for it. And one, might I add, that I admire."

This second compliment was like a sweet caress on Rebel's soul. It was one thing to have her femininity admired. To have her sense of self-esteem appreciated and approved of meant far more to her. She remembered all too well the misery of feeling rejected by the rest of the world, and she had not come by her self-confidence easily. To have someone in Hugh Davenport's position acknowledge her as a person to be reckoned with was balm for a lot of old wounds. And the physical attraction she found so disturbing suddenly took a leap into another dimension of feeling.

She glowed.

He smiled. Really smiled.

Rebel's heart thundered in her ears.

"Would you like a drink?" he asked. "I can recommend the sherry."

"Yes. Thank you."

She gave herself a mental shake as she joined him. Cold, hard sanity insisted that she capitalise on his more mellow mood. Personal interests had to come second place to Celeste.

"And thank you for supporting me against Miss Lumleigh's snobbery," she said as he handed her the glass of sherry.

His gaze lifted, the dark eyes locking onto hers in teasing challenge. "I know how hard you can bite. Perhaps I was protecting *her* from a very formidable adversary."

"No," Rebel said decisively, pushing aside the open invitation for a light and pleasurable flirtation.

One eyebrow lifted. "No?"

"You took my side."

"Perhaps I thought it was the right side."

"So did Celeste."

His face instantly tightened, and the twinkle in his eyes turned to a hard glitter. "You surely don't expect me to condone what she did?"

The abrupt switch of mood and manner upset Rebel's strategy. She tried a soft appeal. "No, I don't. But you could try understanding it, Hugh."

"I understand all too well." It was a curt dismissal of the topic.

Rebel took a deep breath and persisted, unable to accept what was patently untrue. "No, you don't, Hugh. She took my side in a child's way, just as you took my side in an adult's way. What she did was wrong, but the intention behind it was the same as yours."

He lifted his glass in mock salute to her argument. "By all means, see whatever you want to see, Rebel. I beg to differ."

"Why?" she demanded, losing patience with his obtuseness. "Celeste knew I was being taken down and she stopped it. Rudely and crudely. But children aren't masters of subtle finesse."

Aristocratic reserve set in with a vengeance. "That is your interpretation. I have another."

"Well, you're wrong!" Rebel insisted with passionate conviction.

It stirred him into a more vehement response. "Right or wrong, I will not have her behaving like a little savage at my table."

"If you showed her some humanity she wouldn't be a little savage," Rebel retorted fiercely, throwing strategy away and plunging to the heart of the matter.

A mask of cold pride closed over his face. "I have given you a free hand with her. Do what you will." With a stiff little bow he turned away and walked to the fireplace.

Total shut-out.

He stood watching the flames lick over the burning logs, his face a study of dark brooding. It took some time for Rebel to quell her seething frustration. She would win no brownie points by trying to continue an argument with a man who refused to argue, and she didn't know what else to do. She couldn't remember the last time she had felt so at a loss, so paralysed with ineffectiveness.

All her instincts told her that she couldn't feel drawn to a man who was callous and cruel. She was certain in her heart that Hugh Davenport was not a bad person. Nor an unsympathetic one. Yet he had a destructive blind spot where his niece was concerned. It not only had an adverse effect on Celeste. It was eating into him, as well, like a cancer on his soul, souring what should be fine and good.

But how to get rid of it?

If she was to do any lasting good with Celeste, she had to get rid of it. Somehow. The child was too young to stand up against its undermining effect. But if Hugh Davenport wouldn't listen to her, if he kept shutting his mind to even obvious evidence ... Rebel shook her head, swept by a wave of sickening helplessness.

Hugh Davenport chose that moment to swing around and face her, forcing an apologetic smile onto his grim visage. "I should not have agreed to your deal. My better judgment was seduced by—" his smile twisted into a wry grimace "—by a breath of fresh air."

His gaze flickered over her face and hair and down to the soft curves of her body, and Rebel was aware of an intense hunger encompassing her, a desire that was barely kept in check. For several moments she forgot everything else, enthralled by her strong response to the idea of being taken by him, of having every other consideration simply swept away so there were just the two of them, man and woman.

She wanted to know what it would be like to be in his arms, to feel his body pressed to hers, to experience the passion of his kisses. She was sure he would be very passionate. The pent-up feeling that emanated from him was so vibrant it sent waves of rippling heat through her body.

Yet he made no move towards her, no move to pursue what he felt, what he was making her feel. When he finally dragged his gaze to hers, there was a look of black despair in his eyes that clutched at Rebel's heart, squeezing it painfully.

"I realise now that you will end up getting hurt," he said, as though forcing the words from his lips. "And I don't want to see your brightness dimmed. It was selfish of me to want some of it."

Rebel's mind reeled with incredulity. He was choosing to deny whatever there could have been between them!

His voice dropped to a low throb of pained persuasion. "This is no place for you, Rebel. Better for you to leave Celeste to me. Better that you leave tomorrow before—"

"No," she broke in determinedly. "I'm not going, Hugh. Apart from anything else, I can't leave Celeste to you. Not when—"

"Rebel..." He gave her an anguished look. "Believe me, it's for your own good. You must."

"I can't. I don't know why you feel the way you do about Celeste, but to me..." Her eyes begged him to understand. "I see myself in her, Hugh. When I was her age, I was just like her. I—"

"No!" He slammed his glass down so violently on the broad mantelpiece that the stem broke. Crystal shards and sherry spilled onto his hand. He shook them off in careless dismissal and walked towards her with such blazing intensity of purpose that Rebel was mesmerised into immobility, held transfixed by the dark turbulence in his eyes.

He took the glass of sherry from her hand and placed it on the tray. He grasped her upper arms, as though driven to impress his words on her by touch as well as speech. Some deep inner conflict warred briefly on his face, but Rebel was too shaken to decipher the shift of emotions.

"You must listen to me," he said with rasping emphasis. "What you told us at lunch today... I understand why you identify with Celeste. You think of her as having lost her parents like you. But her life does not parallel yours. The loss of her parents is of no significance to Celeste. She did not mourn them as I'm sure you mourned your mother, Rebel. You would not have come here to look at Davenport Hall if you did not remember her with love. That's so, isn't it?"

Her chest was tight, her mouth too dry to speak. She nodded.

"And your adopted family, you love them, too, don't you?"

"Yes," she whispered, hopelessly confused about where this was leading.

"You believe that love can be Celeste's salvation, but that won't happen, Rebel. She'll play with it, manipulate it to her own ends and ultimately throw it back in your face with a contemptuous triumph that will shrivel that giving heart of yours. I know what I'm saying, believe me. God knows she's the cross I have to bear for—" His lips compressed into a savage grimace. "But that's no concern of yours. I shouldn't have let you involve yourself with her."

A bleak resignation settled on his face and dulled his eyes. "For someone like Cynthia Lumleigh, it doesn't really matter. She sees Celeste as nothing more than an annoyance. She would never be deeply wounded by anything Celeste did to her. But you could be, Rebel, because you care too much. And in caring too much, you hand Celeste a weapon that she will use against you."

"No." Mentally and emotionally she recoiled from what he was saying. "No, she needs to be loved. You've got it wrong."

"Rebel." His chest heaved and fell in an impatient sigh. His grasp on her arms tightened momentarily, then fell away. He looked at her with weary cynicism. "Celeste hates me because I see through her games and she knows I see through them. She can't win with me. But you . . ."

His expression softened to one of rueful self-mockery. He lifted a hand and gently stroked her cheek. "To Celeste, love is a weakness to be exploited. If I could convince myself that you would not fall victim to her malicious power games, I would not deny myself the pleasure of knowing you."

His gaze fell to her mouth. His thumb lightly fanned her lower lip. Then, with an air of heavy reluctance, he removed his hand from her face and lifted his eyes to hers.

"But I find that I still have a conscience after all," he said flatly. "And I'm telling you to walk away from this soul-draining battle ground while your ideals are still intact and untarnished."

He knew she felt attracted to him, just as she knew he felt attracted to her. He had just acknowledged it, then withdrawn from it, thereby adding even more force to what he had told her. Because there had been desire in his fingertips, desire in his eyes, desire in the tension that had emanated from him and wound around her like a web of irresistible enthralment. It was still a throbbing reality between them, but with no promise of any future. That had been taken away.

It was another way of saying there was nothing here for her, nothing for her to stay for. Rebel understood that, but was he right about everything else? Had she misled herself over Celeste? She remembered her first impression of the child, her horror at such knowing wickedness. And tonight, that flash of triumphant delight in her blue eyes. Love, a weapon to be used . . .

There was a ponderous knock on the door. It was opened by Brooks.

"Dinner is ready to be served, m'lord," he announced, recalling them both to the set routine of the household.

"Thank you, Brooks," Hugh replied.

The old butler bowed and withdrew.

Hugh turned to Rebel, his shoulders a little straighter as though he was determinedly shrugging off a burden. "Come. We'll talk of more pleasant things," he invited, his lips curving into a dry, whimsical smile. "Of cabbages and kings. Or kangaroos and emu wings."

It teased a wobbly smile from her.

But there was no smile in his dark eyes.

Nor in hers.

CHAPTER SIX

THE DINING ROOM seemed to glow with polished mahogany. The long oval table was set at one end. Gleaming silver placemats took the place of a cloth, and deeply cut crystal glasses accompanied the old and exquisite tableware. At the other end of the table stood a full bowl of pink roses. Overhead, two dimly lit chandeliers cast a soft glow of light around the room.

Brooks held out Rebel's chair for her. The seat was upholstered in velvet brocade, a rose motif worked into a silver-grey background. Rebel noticed. For some reason, it seemed important to notice everything, to imprint a memory that she could recall whenever she wanted to. Yet why she would want to was not easily defined. Perhaps it was part of feeling defeated, of having other more deeply meaningful things ripped away from her. This, at least, would be hers to hold.

Brooks poured white wine. A maid served them freshly cooked asparagus and added a coating of hollandaise sauce.

"Tell me more about this remarkable family of yours," Hugh asked as soon as the servants had left them alone. "I'm intrigued to know how it came about. Was it a deliberate plan of your parents to adopt children from different countries?"

The question barely registered in Rebel's mind. It was, of course, an attempt to get some pretence of normalcy into the evening, a veneer of polite interest to cover the more explosive feelings that still simmered between them.

"Not really. Most of us just happened," Rebel answered offhandedly, her thoughts still revolving in tormenting circles over all of Celeste's actions and responses. She did not doubt that Hugh had spoken what he believed to be the truth, but was it the truth?

"How can so many children—didn't you say fourteen?—just happen?" he queried.

She looked searchingly at the child's uncle. What did he know of children? Couldn't he be wrong about Celeste?

"Have you ever been married, Hugh?" she asked.

He frowned at the abrupt non sequitur to the conversation he had set out to promote. "No." His mouth curled sardonically. "I'm regarded as a very eligible bachelor. Even more so since I inherited my brother's title. And all the worldly goods attached to it. Would you like to marry me?"

The dark eyes derided any suggestion that she might take the question seriously, and the flippant tone of his voice underlined a deep cynicism. Rebel did her best to stifle the queer feeling of disappointment that dragged at her heart.

"I just wondered. Most men of your age are either married or have been," she said non-committally.

"I gather I have been declined," he said with exaggerated self-mockery. "Still, there are any number of candidates for my hand...and bed. Sooner or later I'll choose one and get myself married, if only for the purpose of begetting an heir.''

Was he deliberately trying to shock her? To turn her off him in such a way that there would be no temptation left for her to stay here? Or did his cynicism run so deep that he really meant what he said? The thought of him marrying Cynthia Lumleigh turned Rebel's stomach.

''Wasn't there ever a time when you wanted to get married? To someone you loved?'' she asked, wanting a clearer picture of how his mind was working.

He hesitated. Then the dark eyes locked onto hers, burning with a hard, ruthless light. ''Yes. There was a time when I was blinded enough by sexual attraction to believe I was in love. But fortunately for me, and unfortunately for my brother, the woman who was then the light of my life chose to marry him instead, very quickly revealing herself as a lady of no light at all. Their marriage was not made in heaven. It was certainly no recommendation for the institution.''

Christine...and Celeste was Christine's child! Could his bitter experience with the mother have warped his judgment of the daughter? Yet the child was also his brother's. Didn't that count for anything?

''There is a lot to be said for arranged marriages. Or marriages of convenience,'' he continued with a kind of driven relentlessness, as though he had to convince himself as well as Rebel. ''At least, one's expectations of the union are within the realm of reason. And the disillusionment is cut to a minimum. Much easier to accept.''

He reached for his glass and drank the wine with a haste that suggested he needed to dilute some sour taste in his mouth. Rebel sipped at hers as she tried to sift through what was real and what wasn't. She felt more and more painfully confused by the situation.

"But don't let my jaundiced view of the marital state colour your dreams, Rebel."

The note of sharp concern in his voice drew her gaze to his.

He gave her an ironic smile. "Perhaps there are some marriages made in heaven."

"Yes," she said, thinking of her sister's marriage. She couldn't imagine a happier couple than Tiffany and Joel. Their relationship enriched both their lives in so many immeasurable ways.

Brooks returned to clear away the plates from their first course and top up their glasses with more wine. Rebel couldn't remember having eaten the asparagus, but apparently she had. They were served Dover sole for their main course.

Hugh picked up his glass again, lifting it in a toast to her as he said, "I hope you do marry a man you love and have the family you want."

"Thank you," she returned gravely.

Again he drank with total irreverence for the quality of the wine. Then he attacked the fish on his plate with the air of a man who was determined to stuff it down his throat whether he liked it or not. Rebel picked at hers. She had no appetite at all.

"You didn't answer my earlier question," he reminded her. "About how you and your brothers and sisters came to be adopted into the James family."

"Oh, different times, different places, different circumstances. I'm the sixth eldest, and it was Zachary Lee who found me."

"Zachary Lee?"

"He was the first one adopted. Our parents came across him in New Orleans. He was a child prodigy at chess and was being cruelly exploited by a man who didn't care for anything but what he could make out of Zachary Lee. Our parents rescued him."

"And how did he find you?" Hugh asked curiously.

"He was walking along a street and happened to glance into an alley where I was foraging through garbage bins for something to eat."

"Garbage bins!"

The appalled look on Hugh's face drew a rueful smile from Rebel. "A far cry from your kind of world, Hugh. But it is out there, going on all the time."

"Granted, but why were you doing it?"

"Because I was hungry. I was on the run again at the time."

"On the run from what?"

"From people, mostly. I hated everyone. Just as Celeste does."

"Celeste has never gone hungry in her life." It was a curt dismissal of any comparison between his niece and Rebel. "Didn't anyone take care of you after your mother died?"

"Oh, yes, I was taken care of," Rebel said with savage irony. "All my material needs were met. I was placed with foster parents who took kids in for the government allowance they got for doing so. They housed us, fed us, worked us like slaves and beat us if we didn't do exactly as we were told. I don't think the welfare people realised that. After two years I ran away, and then became a ward of the court.''

She sighed as more memories crawled through her mind, dragging up the feelings that she thought she had recognised in Celeste—the lost feeling of not belonging to anyone, the insecurity of not knowing what the next hour or day or year would bring, the frightening loneliness, the distrust of people in general, the rebellion against uncaring authority.

''I ran away again,'' she continued. ''Eventually I was picked up by the police. I was labelled an uncontrollable child by the welfare people. Unplaceable. Unreachable. Which was fine by me. I knew there wasn't any place for me anyway. I kept running away from wherever they sent me. Even after Zachary Lee found me and took me home with him.''

''How old was he at the time?'' Hugh asked.

''Seventeen.''

He frowned. ''Weren't you frightened of him when he approached you in the street?''

Rebel shook her head, smiling at the absurdity of being frightened of her big brother. ''Zachary Lee is about as big as a person can get without being a bear, but he's also the gentlest person in the world. One look at him and you know you're safe.''

Her eyes softened at the wondrous things he had done for her. ''He promised no-one would hurt me. He gave me chocolate and biscuits and lollies to eat. I had to work hard at winning his respect, but I knew he cared about me because he never lost patience with me and was always there when I needed him. Somehow it was arranged with the authorities that I could stay with the James family. And with Zachary Lee.''

''That's when they adopted you.''

She nodded. ''At first I found it too scary, having a family that really seemed to care what I did and how I felt. I ran away from them a few times. Not very seriously. Just to be independent and test them out. Zachary Lee always found me. He talked me back. In the end, it was really Zachary Lee who made me . . . me!''

''Then he's to be highly commended for all he did,'' Hugh said in a tone of genuine respect. ''I'm sure he's very proud of you.''

''Yes. Yes, he is.'' Her deep love for her wonderful big brother spilled into her voice. ''And I'm proud of him. I'm proud of all my brothers and sisters. Some of them came into the family from far worse circumstances than mine. Our parents taught us how to give each one the feeling of being accepted, no matter what he or she said or did. And gradually the strong network of love and support wound its way around them, bringing the security that made true self expression possible because rejection was no longer an issue. No matter what happens to any of us, there is always the family to fall back on.''

''Then you are rich indeed,'' Hugh remarked softly.

Rebel looked searchingly at him, but there was a bleak hardness on his face that did not invite what she wanted to ask. Yet she had to press the point. ''I was considered unreachable, Hugh. Don't you think there's a chance that I can reach Celeste?''

He didn't even hesitate. "Not a hope in hell. You can't reach people who are without conscience, Rebel. Their minds work on a different plane. There is nothing you can appeal to. Except their self-advantage. But even then they have a twisted view of what their self-advantage is. It's not what you or I think."

"You've only had Celeste in your care for six months, Hugh," Rebel argued. "How can you be so sure?"

He made a harsh, contemptuous sound. "She had a seven-year apprenticeship with her mother, and she is very much her mother's child."

"What about her father? Your own brother. Is there nothing of him in Celeste?"

"Very questionable. Christine deliberately poisoned the relationship I had with my brother by telling him Celeste was my child. She isn't. But whose child she is..." He shrugged. "The father could be any one of a number of lovers. The only certainty is that Christine was her mother."

Rebel was beginning to understand Hugh's hatred of Christine, but she still didn't feel right about him putting Celeste in the same category. The child had obviously been rejected by her nominal father, probably from a very early age. And Rebel doubted that Celeste had spent much time with her mother at all, so Hugh's contention of an apprenticeship carried no great weight. Rebel found it more likely that a woman like Christine wouldn't bother much about a child, and the fact that Celeste had been put in the care of nannies all her life backed up Rebel's opinion that the child had been rejected and neglected by those who should have loved her.

"Forget it, Rebel!" Hugh commanded harshly, as though he had read her thoughts. "You'll only hurt yourself in bashing your head against a brick wall. There's nothing here for you except what you came for. At least I can give you that in return for the trouble you've gone to for the sake of a child."

Rebel was so involved with her concern over Celeste that she didn't immediately grasp Hugh's point. "What do you mean?" she asked.

The conversation was interrupted by the return of Brooks and the maid. Again the plates were cleared, their glasses filled, and they were served with a raspberry souffle.

"We'll have coffee in the library, Brooks," Hugh instructed.

"As you wish, m'lord."

Hugh waited until the servants retired before enlightening Rebel as to his purpose there. "You aren't the first person who has come here in search of what happened to the war orphans, Rebel. This afternoon I remembered there were entries about them in the Hall archives kept in the library. Sir Malcolm Baird found them. I don't know what he wanted them for."

"Who is Sir Malcolm Baird?" Rebel asked curiously.

"A historian. England's leading historian, as a matter of fact," Hugh informed her. "As I recall, he was doing some thesis about displaced persons during the war years. He questioned everyone on the estate and in the village about where the orphans were taken when they left Davenport Hall, but no-one knew."

"I don't suppose the authorities wanted to advertise the fact that they were being shipped to Australia," Rebel dryly observed.

"Certainly there's no note about it in the entries, but I thought you might like to see what was recorded about your mother's stay here."

Rebel's heart lurched as a wave of sadness swept through her. For a moment, the memory of her mother was very vivid; sitting on her bed, stroking Rebel's curls as she spun lovely dreams for her and kissed her goodnight. It could not have been an easy life, raising a child on her own. Sometimes she had cried. It had made Rebel feel all twisted around inside. But her mother would always hug her tight and soothe the fears away. And then one day she had been taken away in an ambulance, and Rebel had never seen her again. But she *had* been here in Davenport Hall all those years ago. There was a written record of it.

"What was your mother's Christian name?" Hugh asked.

"Valerie. Valerie Griffith."

He nodded. "She was definitely here. The orphans' names are listed. There was only the one Griffith."

Rebel blinked away the sudden prickling of tears and swallowed hard to get rid of the lump in her throat. "It was kind of you to look it up for me, Hugh. Thank you. I'd very much like to see all that was written about them."

He grimaced. "There's not much, Rebel. The day they came. The arrangements made for them. The list of names. The day they left."

"It's something," she said simply.

He frowned. "You have nothing from the years with your mother?"

She forced a smile. "Only the memories."

His frown deepened. "I could photocopy the pages if you'd like to have them."

Rebel thought about it, then slowly shook her head. Impersonal records were not a meaningful keepsake. "To see them is enough," she said, lifting her eyes to his.

Her heart lurched again. For once there was no cynicism, no mockery, no proud reserve. Only understanding compassion, a regret that he couldn't do more, a wish that things were different. Then as if suddenly vexed with himself, a grim anger swept his face of any softness and he looked down, picked up his spoon and dug into the souffle.

Rebel followed suit, but she felt so tight and tremulous inside she found it difficult to swallow the sweet, even though it melted in her mouth. There was no future with him, she kept reminding herself, yet the rest of her felt in turbulent rebellion against that edict. Somehow the whole situation was wrong.

Celeste...

This man who did have a kind and sympathetic heart...

Yet he had closed it against his niece.

And was closing it to her, as well.

The distant reserve was in full force when he politely inquired if she was ready to leave the table, but she sensed a tightly coiled tension in him as he escorted her to the library. She was intensely aware of his closeness while he stood beside her at the central desk, pointing out the entries in the leather-bound journal, a day-to-day diary for 1944. Yet not by word or manner did he deviate from the role of courteous and considerate host.

The orphans had occupied the second floor of Davenport Hall, which was traditionally the children's floor, Hugh informed her. Celeste had only been brought down to the first floor when one of her nannies had complained that the stairs were too much for her.

"Would you mind if I had a look around the second floor?" Rebel asked. "If I wouldn't be disturbing anyone."

"There's no-one to disturb. The staff's rooms are on the floor above it. When you finish your coffee I'll take you up."

He seemed set on fulfilling any hopes she might have had in coming to Davenport Hall in search of a piece of her mother's life. As he escorted her from room to room on the second floor, Rebel recalled that this was precisely what she had wanted from him yesterday, before Celeste had burst onto the scene and changed everything.

It felt strange to think that had only been yesterday. Time seemed to have expanded or lengthened, spanning far more than a fixed number of hours. Perhaps it was all the talk of the past and the future, the memories and emotions stirred, the confusion raised by what was right and wrong.

It felt stranger still when Hugh showed her the schoolroom. The bedrooms had not struck any personal chord for her. They seemed empty of any sense of ever having been occupied by a lot of children. But no sooner had Rebel stepped into the schoolroom than she was assailed by an eerie feeling of timelessness, and the phantom presence of generations of children crowded in on her.

Her mother had played in here, taken picture books from the shelves, sat curled on one of the window seats, drawn on the blackboard with sticks of chalk, had her turn on the old wooden rocking horse in the corner—a little girl with brown curls and hazel eyes and no-one left in the world to love her.

Tears welled in Rebel's eyes, and this time she couldn't blink them back. She reached out and ran her fingers over the scarred lid of an old desk. Ink stains, pencil scribbles, indentations, scratches...

"That was my desk," Hugh said behind her, a whimsical reminiscence in his voice.

"And others' before you," Rebel murmured huskily, knowing that it was older than Hugh, far older.

She didn't hear him move, yet somehow when he turned her gently towards him she wasn't surprised. She didn't see the expression on his face because her eyes were too blurred by tears, but there was warmth and comfort and tenderness in the arms that wound around her and held her close to him. It felt good to lean on his strength, to rest her head on his shoulder. It soothed the empty ache inside her.

"I'm sure your mother was happy here, Rebel," he said gruffly. "This was a happy place once. My brother and I..." His chest rose and fell in a deep sigh. "We had a lot of fun in this schoolroom. I wish..."

Again he broke off, perhaps lost in memories that were suddenly very poignant to him. One of his hands slid up her back, and she felt the slight tug of fingers raking slowly through the tumbled silk of her curls. He rubbed his cheek very softly against her hair, and maybe she imagined it, but she thought his mouth brushed her ear.

It was then she became aware the desire to comfort was changing into a desire for another kind of intimacy. Warmth simmered into a more electric heat. Strength gathered a harder tension. An excitement began to stir in the pit of her stomach. Rebel knew in her head that to stay passively in his embrace was flirting with danger, yet some wantonly reckless part of her whispered that it had always been meant to be, so why not let it? Why not?

"You have a family to go back to, Rebel," Hugh argued in a low, pained voice. "A fine family who love you. Looking back to times gone past—it doesn't do any good."

His hand curled around the nape of her neck and lifted her head back. Rebel opened tear-heavy eyes. His face looked tight and strained. "Your mother would want you to go on from here, making the best of your life. Tomorrow, when you go back to London—"

"No!" she cried, every instinct shrieking loud and insistent rebellion against his decision. It was wrong.

It had to be wrong. "I can't go, Hugh," Rebel choked out.

Again his chest rose and fell and she saw his face contort with savage frustration. "What more do I have to say to make you see it's useless?" he demanded harshly.

Rebel swallowed hard. She didn't really understand it herself, but the decision had been made for her in this schoolroom. However wrong she might be, she couldn't turn her back on a lost child with no-one to love her. And she couldn't bear to let this man turn his back on her with nothing resolved between them. Her feeling that there was something very positive to be explored, something too strong to push aside.

"I have to try," she whispered, her eyes pleading with his for a stay of judgment. "You agreed on a week, Hugh."

His jaw clenched. The dark eyes glittered at her with such violence of feeling that a frisson of fear ran down Rebel's spine. His hands moved to her upper arms, gripped hard, his fingers kneading her flesh in tortured indecision. Then he pushed her away from him, forcibly holding her at arm's length.

"Then on your head be it," he grated accusingly. "I won't answer for what happens."

He left her there, striding away as though the hounds of hell were biting at his heels. And Rebel was so shaken by the dark violence of his departure that she did not move for a long time.

There was some influence here at Davenport Hall, she thought, some power that went beyond anything she had ever faced in her life before. She felt she was somehow caught up in a fight between good and evil.

Her parents, her family had taught her that good always triumphed in the end—if you believed in it enough.

CHAPTER SEVEN

REBEL DID NOT SPEND a restful night. It was difficult to dismiss Hugh's opinion of his niece. It was just as difficult to dismiss how she felt about him. The attraction was no longer without any substance. She felt drawn to him in ways she had never experienced with any other man. Yet she had to face the fact that he had rejected any further interest in her, wiping his hands of the whole situation.

The thought that maybe she should do the same kept gnawing away at Rebel's mind, making her doubt her own instincts. But a week of her life was not much to give, she argued to herself. If she truly wasn't needed or wanted here, she would know by then, and she could go away with a clear conscience.

Her reasoning, however, was continually mocked by the feeling she would never be clear of Davenport Hall. Somehow this place had staked a claim on her that she couldn't shake off.

Rebel went down to breakfast early the next morning. She had a business appointment in London at eleven o'clock, and she wanted to see Celeste before she left. The need to test the rapport she thought she had established yesterday was uppermost in Rebel's mind, but there was also the need to reinforce it this morning if she was right in trusting her own experience against Hugh's.

Bracing herself to face both antagonists, Rebel felt extremely tense as she entered the informal dining room. Sunlight streamed through the long windows, making the white and yellow room look so bright and cheerful that it mocked the idea of anything dark at Davenport Hall. But any such deception was quickly dispensed with as the only occupant of the breakfast table lifted her face to Rebel.

The flash of welcome in the little girl's eyes died a quick death as they took in the smart green business suit Rebel wore. "I knew you'd go away," Celeste said flatly, and turned her attention to the cereal she was eating, digging her spoon so hard into the bowl that a few cornflakes leapt onto the table.

"I'm not going away, but I'm not a lady of leisure like you," Rebel said as she walked to the chair opposite Celeste's. "I've got work to do. Maybe, if you're good enough, I'll take you with me someday."

Rebel sat down and poured herself a glass of orange juice from the jug on the table, not even glancing at the child as she did so, although she felt the hard scrutiny Celeste was giving her.

A maid came in and inquired what Rebel would like for breakfast. Bacon and eggs and toast would be fine, Rebel told her with a broad smile, hoping that it would serve as a positive proof that nothing was amiss with her this morning.

"What work have you got to do?" Celeste demanded to know.

Rebel transferred the smile to her. "I told you about the balloon race yesterday," she said brightly. "I still need to get thirty-three more sponsors and I hope I'll clinch one of those today. So I have to go to London to talk to the person I've got lined up and persuade him into signing."

Celeste looked unconvinced. The big blue eyes glowered with suspicion.

Rebel widened her smile to a reassuring grin. "I'll tell you if I've succeeded when you get home from school this afternoon. That's if you want to know."

"I'm not going to school!" Celeste stated truculently. "I hate school! I'm never going back there!"

Back to square one, Rebel thought, and girded herself to start all over again. "That's tough, kid!" she said sympathetically. "I guess you're going to miss out on a lot of learning."

The return to "kid" brought a mutinous look to the blue eyes. "I don't care!" It was a predictable retort.

Rebel shrugged. "Well, it's your decision. No business of mine. Personally, I'd hate all those other kids knowing they could beat me at everything just because they've learnt more than I have. But if you hate school that much, I guess you'd rather be stupid, anyway."

Rebel's breakfast made a timely arrival, and she gave all her attention to eating it, leaving Celeste to chew over those remarks. She couldn't very well insist that the child go to school. That would turn her into one of the enemy. On the other hand, she didn't want to leave Celeste alone all day, either. That would not be helpful at all. Which meant Rebel had another problem on her plate.

She was pouring herself a cup of coffee when Celeste finally broke the silence.

"I can't go back to that old school anyway. They told Uncle Hugh they wouldn't have me there anymore." The defiance didn't quite cover an uncertain quiver in her voice.

"Is that right?" Rebel wondered if this was the first school that Celeste had been expelled from, but she kept her voice light and casual as she rambled on. "Sounds like you messed up, kid. But I'm sure your Uncle Hugh could find you another school if you wanted him to. Maybe one you wouldn't hate at all. There are lots of schools. Though I guess if you keep messing up enough, you might run out of them."

Celeste frowned over that thought for a few moments. "I'm not asking Uncle Hugh for anything!" she said, planting her elbows on the table and pushing her fists into her cheeks.

Rebel shook her head. "You're going to miss an awful lot of years of learning. But that's your problem. I was just thinking, since you're not going to school today, how about coming up to London with me? I've only got one meeting and that shouldn't take too long. And then we could grab some hamburgers and chips and take a boat ride down the Thames."

The blue eyes lit up like stars. "Truly? Could we?"

"I don't see why not." Rebel quelled her own wild leap of joy at this response. She narrowed her eyes, to all intents and purposes giving the matter serious consideration. "Of course, you'll have to be patient while

I'm in my meeting. No stamping on anyone's toes or yelling or carrying on or being frightful. And there's plenty you could learn from me. Better than a university education. But it is important to me that I succeed. So, if you mess up, kid, I'll never take you to work with me again."

"I promise I won't mess up, Rebel," she said earnestly. "Double triple promise!"

If Rebel had needed any further assurance that the little girl was not the monster Hugh had insisted she was, it was embodied in those childish words, and in the almost desperate eagerness to grasp the chance Rebel was holding out to her.

Rebel knew it was important to accept the promise without question. Trust was built on trust. She smiled. "Okay, then. You'd better go and get ready. I'll tell Mrs. Tomkins you're coming with me so your Uncle Hugh knows where you are and won't worry about you."

"He won't care!" Celeste cried as she ran for the door.

It was said with such absolute certainty that Rebel's heart twisted. The terrible part was she could not deny it was true. And how to change Hugh Davenport's attitude around was going to be the most critical problem of all in this rescue mission.

However, Rebel's renewed confidence over the little girl received a setback when she sought out Mrs. Tomkins to apprise her of the plan for today. The housekeeper almost wrung her hands in agitation at hearing that Rebel was taking Celeste to London. Her pale blue eyes widened in horror when Rebel also dropped the fact that the trip involved business as well as pleasure.

"Far be it from me to interfere, Miss James, but I think you should discuss it with Lord Davenport first," she advised anxiously. "Lady Celeste... Well, she can seem like an angel when she wants something, but... Oh, dear! I don't think you should risk your business with her, Miss James. I really don't. There's no telling..."

Mrs. Tomkins pulled herself up, took a deep breath and retreated into discretion. "It's not for me to say. Let me take you to Lord Davenport, Miss James. He's in his office. It's just down the hallway past the library. I'm sure he wouldn't want you to, uh..."

"Lord Davenport has already told me I can do anything I wish with Celeste, Mrs. Tomkins," Rebel said firmly, although the housekeeper's flutters had stirred a nervous flutter in her stomach.

It was unsettling to discover that Hugh's opinion of Celeste was shared by others who lived under the same roof. Rebel could hardly excuse Mrs. Tomkins's judgment as having been warped by some past experience with the child's mother, and her concern was obviously deep and genuine.

"I don't think you understand, Miss James," she protested worriedly. "Here at the Hall is one thing. The staff are all, ah, used to Lady Celeste's ways. Although no-one noticed her locking the nanny in the gazebo. But no real harm was done."

"Precisely. And no harm will be done today, Mrs. Tomkins," Rebel said with more confidence than she actually felt. The memory of welfare workers who had never understood her was a help in boosting her determination to follow her own judgment. Even the most well-meaning people could mistake rebellion for wickedness.

"Lord Davenport knows what I'm about," she assured the housekeeper. "I'm just extending him the courtesy of informing him that his niece is spending the day with me in London, if you'd be so kind as to pass on that message at an opportune time."

Despite the authority with which she spoke, Rebel could not help feeling some apprehension about her business appointment. She *was* taking a gamble with Celeste. However, with only a week to work a recognisable miracle, gambles had to be taken, she reasoned. Besides, even if her trust in the child was misplaced, it wasn't the end of the world if she lost today's sponsorship.

As it turned out, however, the day could not have been more rewarding. Not only did Rebel get the targeted sponsorship tied up, but by stressing the prestige of the event and subtly dropping the fact that there was a lot of fun to be had out of friendly competition, she persuaded the company director to use the old-school-tie network to introduce her to a few more sponsors. He even offered to make contact for her and set up interviews. Which, of course, Rebel accepted with charm and grace.

She suspected that having the Earl of Stanthorpe's niece with her was a considerable asset in this instance. Rebel found it ironically amusing that an ingrained class snobbery worked to her advantage on this occasion. And it certainly hadn't hurt that Celeste had been absolutely angelic throughout the whole meeting, listening to everything with rapt attention.

Rebel, therefore, was in particularly high spirits when they left the building. "We've got it in the bag. Another sponsorship on its way, and almost certainly two more, as well. Thirty more to go," she whispered exultantly to Celeste, who grinned at her, delighted to be Rebel's confidante about her work.

They had all sorts of junk food for lunch to celebrate the success, and then they cruised down the Thames to Greenwich. For the first time, Celeste acted like a completely normal little girl, excited, interested, responsive to everything around her and chattering away to Rebel nineteen to the dozen.

Perhaps Rebel's spontaneous delight at seeing all the historic landmarks along the Thames had its influence on the child. The sense of sharing real enjoyment had its own magic. They laughed at the jokes made by the guide whose commentary was pure entertainment. At Greenwich they toured the *Cutty Sark*, marvelling at how sailors had lived for months on end in such cramped quarters. They ate ice-creams on the trip to the pier near Big Ben.

Rebel had instructed the chauffeur to pick them up there, and when they climbed the steps to the street, the black Rolls-Royce was waiting for them. For a moment Celeste baulked at getting into the car. She shot a look at Rebel that said more clearly than words that she wanted to run away and never go back to Davenport Hall. But that meant running away from Rebel, as well, and her need for the caring and sharing Rebel offered her overrode everything else.

She slumped dejectedly on the back seat. Rebel settled beside her, then put her arm around the little girl and cuddled her close. "Tired?" she murmured, dropping a kiss on the top of her silky blonde head.

Celeste heaved a deep sigh. "Do we have to go home?" she asked plaintively.

"There's always another day," Rebel answered, giving her a quick hug. "We don't want to worry your uncle by staying out too late."

"He won't care," came the unhappy mutter.

"I think he would, Celeste," Rebel said seriously, wanting to give the child at least that little bit of security, even though she herself was unsure of it.

I'll make him care, she silently vowed. All the doubts Hugh had seeded in her mind last night had been swept away today. Celeste was no monster. She was simply a child in desperate need of some real loving. Somehow her uncle had to be shown that.

"Rebel?"

"Mmm?"

Celeste lifted her face, the big blue eyes filled with yearning appeal. "Could you adopt me into your family? It wouldn't matter if there was another English one, would there? You've got two from India and two from Korea."

A deep sadness savaged Rebel's heart. It was a solution but she couldn't see the Earl of Stanthorpe accepting it.

She smiled. "I'm sure all my brothers and sisters would love having another English one, Celeste, but my parents can't adopt children who already have a home and family. That's not how it works. You belong with your uncle.''

"But he doesn't want me."

Rebel was plunged into murky waters. She picked her words slowly and with enormous care.

"Celeste, your uncle has never had children of his own. I don't think he knows how to go about looking after a girl of your age. He tried to get you nannies because he thought that was best for you. I'm sure he doesn't understand why you keep getting rid of them, and it makes him angry because he doesn't know what else to try."

Rebel paused to let that sink in, then softly added, "Have you ever tried telling him what you want him to do?''

"*He* wouldn't listen," Rebel decided sulkily.

"He asked me to stay at Davenport Hall because he thought you might like it," Rebel reminded her, deciding that this one lie was justified. "I think if you try talking to your uncle, he might understand things a lot better."

She snuggled the child closer to her and started stroking her hair as she spoke in a soft, soothing voice. "Some people care a lot inside. They just don't know how to show it. Remember what I told you yesterday? Some people laugh to cover up. Or say silly things. Others frown and look stern. Like your uncle. Getting mad at them doesn't change anything. It only makes things worse. But if you try to be different with them, it gives them a chance to be different. I think that's always worth trying.''

The only response was another sigh. Rebel kept stroking her hair. She didn't know what else to say.

The child fell asleep on the drive to Davenport Hall. Rebel decided she had to tackle Hugh Davenport again, and do it before Celeste's bedtime. Another one of those chilly goodnights from him, and any slim hope she had kindled in Celeste's heart would be killed stone dead.

They had no sooner returned to the Hall when Rebel was presented with the opportunity she wanted. Brooks opened the front door for them. "Miss James. Lady Celeste," he addressed them in his ultra-dignified manner. "M'lord asked that you see him upon your return."

Rebel instantly swung a smile to Celeste. "You see? Your uncle was worried about us. He must have thought we'd be home much earlier. I'll go and assure him we're fine. Since it's almost time for your tea, you'd better hop on out to the kitchen."

She lifted the smile to the butler. "Where is Lord Davenport, Brooks?"

"In his office, I believe, Miss James."

"I'll come up to your room at bedtime, Celeste," Rebel promised her, and hurried down the hall, intent on smashing Hugh's prejudice against his niece.

There was no answer to her knock on the office door. Unsure whether she had come to the right room or not, Rebel opened the door to check. Her gaze quickly swept around a very workmanlike study that held a great deal of office equipment, including a personal computer. The man she sought occupied a winged leather chair centred behind a huge desk, but turned towards the long windows beyond it.

"Yes?" he asked wearily, not looking to see who had entered.

Rebel took a deep breath, steeling herself for the confrontation that she had to win. "You wanted to see me, Hugh," she stated evenly.

He came out of his chair in one swift, lithe movement, his head jerking towards her, his eyes stabbing across the distance between them. The blaze of sheer relief sweeping from him and enveloping her made Rebel catch her breath. His gaze swept swiftly down the figure-hugging green suit as he stepped forward, around the desk, bringing himself closer to her. He seemed to pull himself to a halt, hands clenching and unclenching in some agitation of spirit. His face settled into severe, grim lines.

He was dressed less formally than she had ever seen him before, grey slacks and a dark blue turtleneck sweater, which left no doubt about his impressive physique. It fitted him so snugly that the musculature of his shoulders and arms gave a telling emphasis to his masculinity. His thick black hair was slightly mussed, as though he had raked his fingers through it. For some reason it made him look more human, and more compellingly attractive.

One of his hands jerked out in an awkward little gesture. "You made it back." His voice was uncharacteristically rough, almost gravelly.

"Of course."

"There's no of course about it," he snapped at her. "After all that I've told you, it was madness to take that child with you today. I know I said you could do as you liked with her, but..." He shook his head, dragged in a deep breath and produced a calmer voice. "I accept the blame for that. Just tell me the extent of the damage and I'll do what I can to repair it."

Rebel frowned at him in puzzlement. "What damage are you talking about?"

He grimaced in angry impatience. "There's no point in covering up, Rebel. It's going to keep on happening. I know all too well that Celeste wreaks havoc wherever she goes. Just tell me what she did and I'll do my best to smooth over whatever business she wrecked for you."

Rebel burned. She forgot all about even-tempered reasoning. "That's right!" she flashed at him bitterly. "Condemn her unheard! Think the worst of her! That's what you've done all along, isn't it? Never giving her a chance!"

The accusations took the wind out of his sails, and Rebel flew into attack. "I trusted your niece to be a model of decorum while I transacted my business today, and she didn't let me down! I doubt that any other child could have been better behaved. In fact, she was so good and so full of eager interest that she helped me get two more prospects for sponsorships. I'd have no hesitation in taking her anywhere with me. And you know what the secret of that is?"

She didn't wait for an answer. She knew he didn't have the right one. "It's simply to want her with you," she said with blistering scorn for his judgment. "To genuinely want her to be with you. Every child responds to that, Hugh Davenport. They want to be wanted. And Celeste is no different than any other child. Except she's never been wanted by anyone. And whose fault is that? Is it her fault that she wasn't born to parents who would love her? Is it her fault that she was passed on to a man who judges her by her mother?"

"With good reason," he bit out, the dark eyes bitterly warring with her scorn.

Rebel wasn't accepting that. Not anymore. Like a tigress defending her cub, the claws came out and struck, intent on drawing blood. Her nose flared, her eyes glittered, and every word she spoke was designed to stab into his conscience.

"Well, you just stop and ask yourself why Celeste acts the way she does around you. Because I'll tell you how she acted this afternoon with me! We had fun together. The kind of fun that children should have. The kind of fun that her parents should have given her. And didn't! The kind of fun you should give her in place of her parents. And don't! The kind of fun that nannies should have been encouraged to give her. And weren't! And it was like she was in heaven for the first time in her life!"

"I don't doubt it! Even the spawn of the devil might relish a taste of heaven, just for the sheer novelty of it!"

The savagery of the reply stunned Rebel into shocked silence. She stared at her antagonist as though he had just grown horns.

"You obviously held out a carrot she fancied and she gobbled it up," he mocked.

Rebel's eyes flared with furious contempt. "Yes! No doubt it was a novelty. Since all she's ever got has been the rough end of the stick. I'm coming to see that you're the monster, Hugh Davenport. Not your niece.''

''A monster, am I?'' He wheeled and snatched up a sheaf of papers from his desk. He shook them at her as he walked towards her, biting out every word as though he begrudged it. ''I have spent most of today contacting the top winegrowers of France and Germany, canvassing them to be sponsors of your balloon race. They have agreed to a meeting with you. In Paris. On Friday week.''

He picked up her hand and slapped the papers into it. ''There are the names and the homework you should do on them before talking business.'' The dark eyes seared hers with blazing anger. ''And that, Miss Rebel Griffith James, was done to save you from your stubborn foolhardiness and Celeste's destructiveness. You can thank your lucky stars that she decided to play your game today. I can only say God help you if you take such a risk again!''

His closeness and the violence of feeling emanating from him set Rebel's nerves on edge. But nothing was going to make her back off now. ''Is this supposed to buy me off?'' she snapped at him.

''Quit while you're ahead, Rebel,'' he grated.

''And leave Celeste to your tender mercies?'' Her legs felt shaky but she stepped past him, walked over to his desk, tossed the papers on it, then turned to face him, a proud contempt stamped on her face. ''I don't need your patronage. I can make it on my own.''

''Don't be a damned fool!'' he exploded.

"You presume too much, Hugh Davenport!" Rebel fired at him. "Just as you've done with Celeste."

His lips thinned as he fought to regain control. He jerked to the door, opened it, stood back, then shot her a blistering look. "Go your own way to damnation, then! There's no talking sense to you."

"I'm not finished!" Rebel bit the words out in defiant determination.

He shut the door again and faced her with an air of exaggerated patience. Rebel glared at him, resolving to dent the brick wall of his prejudice if it was the last thing she ever did. She took a deep breath and started again.

"Have you ever once reached out to that child? Taken her hand in affection? Taken her in your arms for a hug? Or even given her a perfunctory kiss goodnight?"

The look of revulsion on his face was answer enough.

"No. I thought not."

"One can hardly feel affection for a child of her nature," he said coldly.

Rebel grimly held onto her temper. "Her nature was formed by rejection, Hugh. And you have contributed to it by withholding any form of bonding with her."

"Form a bond with Christine's child?" He gave a harsh, derisive laugh.

Rebel battled the red haze that threatened to cloud her mind again. "No child should be judged by her parents," she argued vehemently. "For all I know, my father could have been a cruel, malicious murderer. That doesn't make me one."

His face tightened. He gave her a wintry look that should have chilled her to the bone. "Have you quite finished?"

Rebel stuck to her guns. "No, I haven't. You said last night you still have a conscience. I think you'd better start examining it, because you're wrong about Celeste. You're very badly wrong. And if you don't start admitting that possibility and give her a chance to show that you're wrong—" Rebel shook her head "—God help her, because you're the monster."

He stared at her stonily, making no comment.

Rebel searched for more ammunition but everything seemed futile. She heaved a defeated sigh. He had declared his niece unreachable last night, but he was the unreachable one. "I'll spare us all the hypocritical exercise of bringing Celeste to you to say goodnight," she said sadly. "You obviously don't mean it, and I don't want to spoil the one good day she's had with a false note."

No response.

She gave up and walked towards the door, her legs dragging in defeat. It seemed wrong that he still had the power to attract her, to touch something inside her that made her stop and look at him, her eyes searching the hard, relentless mask of his face. Last night she had thought him a good man. A sympathetic man. A kind man.

Without any conscious thought she reached up and softly laid her palm on his cheek. "How could I be so wrong about you?'' she whispered huskily, her eyes reflecting the silent anguish of her soul.

The gentle touch—perhaps the words—cracked something inside him. His cheek contracted under her palm. His breath rushed from his lips in a hiss. A dangerous glitter burned in his eyes.

"Damn you!" he rasped. "Don't you know when to stop?"

He snatched her hand from his cheek but held it in midair, his fingers dragging over hers, kneading flesh and bone. For several nerve-tearing moments there was a grimly fought battle on his face, but the crack in his control kept widening. With a half stifled groan he reached out and scooped her body hard against his. He released her hand and thrust his fingers through the tumbled mass of her hair. His eyes blazed into hers—desire, demand, need—coming closer, closer, his mouth tasting hers, sensuously, seductively, greedily.

His arm tightened around her, pressing her closer, enveloping her with a dominance that struck some deep chord of primitive woman inside Rebel. Her thighs quivered against the power of his. Her stomach churned and melted around the hardness that commanded her submission. Her breasts ached with tender sensitivity, crushed against the pulsing warmth of his chest. And her arms slid around his neck, wantonly responding to her possessive urges.

She had desperately wanted to reach him and she would. Yes, she would. Down to the innermost depths of his being. She would wrench every last ounce of control from him and force him to accept all that she was and everything that entailed.

He stormed her mouth with a passion that would not, could not be denied, and it was an invasion that she welcomed, exulted in and returned with a fierce recklessness. But somewhere it went wrong—or right—and all she had ever known before spun on its axis and moved into a different dimension of feeling.

Somewhere in the back of her mind was a blinding recognition that *this* was what her life had been leading up to. All the years she had spent weaving the character and personality that was so individually hers wavered into an insubstantial haze. The only pounding reality was the wild sense of belonging to this man who held her, whose hunger for her she recklessly fed, whose need was her need, whose desire was her desire.

His lips left hers and grazed over her ear, caressing, whispering into her dazed mind. "Come away with me. France, Spain, Italy... I'll take you anywhere you want..."

Rebel was so intoxicated with the promise of what she could share with this man that it was difficult to think. It took her several moments to grasp what was wrong. "Celeste—"

"Forget her!" he commanded harshly.

"I can't!" she cried in painful protest. How could she forget a child who was so much like the lost child she had been?

He drew back. He cradled her face in his hands. His eyes bored into hers with urgent intensity. "Let her go, Rebel. She can only come between us."

"Won't you give her a chance? Please, Hugh? Please?" she begged, torn by the dual claims on her heart.

His face twisted in anguish. "For God's sake! Don't let her do this to you!" Again his eyes bored their dark, riveting demand. "We can have something, Rebel. You want it as much as I do. Just come away with me and—"

"No!" She wrenched her face out of his grasp and dredged up the strength to step back. "We can't have anything, ever." Her voice trembled with the sense of loss that burrowed through her, but she couldn't do what she knew to be wrong, however much she wanted it to be right. "I can't—I won't feel anything for a man who refuses to give a child a chance."

Then, before he could do or say anything more to tempt her into weakening, she lunged past him, opened the door and fled. He called her name but she didn't stop. She didn't stop until the door of her room shut out the rest of Davenport Hall. And then she flung herself onto the four-poster bed and burst into tears.

CHAPTER EIGHT

REBEL WAS NOT given to tears. Not on her own account, anyway. However, she had never before tasted a dream that had promised so much, only to have it torn away from her and thrust beyond her reach. It had been a long, long time since she had felt so vulnerable to hurt, but the hurt now was so devastating, she could barely contain it.

Yet she had to.

Celeste was expecting a bedtime story, and Rebel would not let her down. It could undo all the progress that had been made today. Although some of that would be inevitably destroyed by the little girl's uncle, Rebel thought despairingly.

Nevertheless, she couldn't present herself to the child in the mess she was in, which meant she had to pull herself together and get on with the job, regardless of her own feelings. She was no quitter. No matter what Hugh Davenport said or did, she was going to stand by Celeste and see the child through to a solid set of positive principles.

The little girl was sitting up in bed waiting for her when Rebel entered her room. The glow of anticipation on her face made Rebel's smile a little less forced. She managed to put enough zest into her story about the drover's dog that Celeste was giggling helplessly when it came to the part where the drover insisted he wouldn't have his injuries tended to until the doctor treated the dog's injuries first.

"'That there dog is more human than you, Doctor,' the drover growled," Rebel went on, much to Celeste's gurgling delight, and when the story finished, the little girl was still laughing as Rebel gathered her up for a big hug.

Then suddenly the laughter choked off and the pliant body in her arms stiffened. Rebel didn't need to look around to know what had happened to change the happy atmosphere. Her body tensed and she had to fight for composure.

What did it mean? Had Hugh changed his mind? Was he about to give Celeste a chance? Or had he come to challenge Rebel's judgment of his niece, to prove that she was wrong and he was right?

Rebel fiercely prayed that he would try to be openminded, that this meant he was willing to review the situation. Her heart was pounding chaotically as her mind raced over how to get Celeste in the right frame of mind to meet her uncle halfway. So much could hang on the next few minutes. So much that Rebel was frightened to even consider the possible outcomes.

Still cradling Celeste against her shoulder, she turned her head and injected a bright, welcoming note into her voice. "Here's your uncle come to see you. I guess he wants to hear what you've been doing today."

She smoothly laid the child down on her pillow, tucked the bedclothes around her and dropped a kiss on her forehead. Celeste stared fixedly at her uncle. The big blue eyes had lost all their twinkle.

"Hey!" Rebel called softly. "Don't I get a kiss back?"

Celeste looked at her in a kind of panic-stricken appeal, then almost defiantly she gave Rebel a fierce peck on the cheek and dropped straight down, her eyes glaring at her uncle as though daring him to find fault with her.

"Goodnight, Celeste," Rebel said quietly.

The benediction was not returned. Rebel doubted that Celeste even heard it. Her whole attention was wound up with waiting to see what her uncle was going to say or do.

He had not yet moved from his position just inside the doorway. Rebel steeled herself to face him in as natural a manner as possible, then rose from the bed and walked towards him, a smile pasted firmly on her lips.

"I'll leave you together," she said lightly.

The strained expression on his face did not bode well for any breaking of the ice between him and his niece. The dark eyes flashed Rebel a savage challenge that eroded the hope of any truce in their battle. But the scene was set. There was no choice now but to let it play its course.

He fixed a smile on his face in mocking response to hers. "Thank you," he said, stepping aside to let her pass through the doorway.

He did not close the door after her, for which Rebel was grateful. It enabled her to stand out of sight in the hallway and still be able to hear what passed between the two antagonists. She had no guilt at all about eavesdropping. If the encounter went badly, she needed to know so that she could repair any damage done. At least, that was what she told herself. But her whole body was aching with a desperate hope for a miracle to happen, a miracle that would breathe life into promises for the future.

"I hear you've had quite a big day in London," Hugh started, inviting a response.

None came.

"Did you have a good time, Celeste?"

"Yes." Defiantly.

"What did you do?" A light note of interest in his voice.

Rebel felt almost dizzy with relief. He was trying. At least on the surface. She willed Celeste to respond.

"We sold a sponsorship for the balloon race and got two more in the bag." This was said both belligerently and boastfully. "Then we ate junk food and had a boat ride under all the bridges."

A pause. Rebel held her breath, wondering what Hugh Davenport would make of that. Undoubtedly Celeste was expecting criticism and was preparing to make a fierce retaliation when it came.

"Sounds like it was a lot of fun."

Rebel could almost feel Celeste's surprise. She wouldn't be sure how to react, and when the response came, predictably it was another show of defiance.

"I can learn more from Rebel than I can from any old school. Even from a university!"

Rebel winced as she heard her own casual words being tossed back at her. Kids picked up the silliest statements, twisted their meaning.

"Perhaps you're right. Maybe you will."

The dry concession was totally unexpected, even by Rebel. Her heart clenched.

Silence. The whisper of a deep sigh. Then, very softly, "Goodnight, Celeste."

No reply.

Rebel sagged with disappointment. If only Celeste had responded more positively.

"Uncle Hugh..." Thin and uncertain.

"Yes, Celeste?" His voice was closer to the doorway.

No answer.

"Is there something you want?" Perhaps a slight thread of kindness there.

"Can I have a dog?" A breathy little rush.

"A dog?"

Rebel's heart sank. There was a frown in his voice. Give her a dog, her mind screamed at him.

"Would you look after it, Celeste?" Uncertainty in his voice. "I wouldn't feel right..."

"I'd look after it, Uncle Hugh. I really truly promise. If it got hurt I'd get a doctor, and I wouldn't let anyone put it out in any old yard, and I'd make sure it got fed even before I eat myself. It could sleep on my bed and..."

The desperately eager words tumbled over themselves, and Rebel couldn't help smiling at the way Celeste had taken the story of the drover's dog to heart. She hoped that her uncle had the heart to respond.

"Well, if it's to live in the house," he said slowly, "perhaps a Yorkshire terrier would be best."

"You mean you'll let me have one?" Fearful hope.

"I don't see why not. I'll telephone some kennels tomorrow and see if any are for sale. If so, I'll make an appointment for us to see them. We'll go together so that you can choose the one you want."

Rebel heaved a huge sigh of relief. He was taking more than a forced step. He was trying hard. There was hope for the future.

"*You'll* take me?" The little girl couldn't quite bring herself to believe it.

There was a slight pause, then a firm, "Yes. I'll take you, Celeste. That's a promise."

There was another longish silence.

"Uncle Hugh?" Barely audible. "Rebel said..."

"Mmm? What did Rebel say?" His voice was farther away again. He was moving back to the bed.

"She said you should hug and kiss goodnight so you can forget all the bad things that have happened before you go to sleep."

"That sounds good. I guess no-one ever taught me that."

"It's not very hard to learn."

There was an excruciating pause before Hugh responded. "It would be nice to forget the bad things. Would you like to tell me how to go about it?"

"Well, I put my arms around your neck like this. And then you put your arms around me and hold tight."

"Like this?"

"Yes. And then you sort of rub your cheek over my hair."

"Like this?"

The ensuring little silence bore its own message.

Rebel knew all she needed to know. Anything more was an intrusion.

If he had needed any proof that his niece was no more nor less than a vulnerable little child, aching to be accepted and loved, he had it now. And to his credit, he had responded, however difficult it had been for him. No matter how deep the darkness lurking in his soul, he was essentially a good and decent man. With a heart. And a conscience.

She crept down the hallway to her room, her heart too full, her composure far too brittle to face Hugh Davenport until she had herself firmly under control. It would be soon enough to face him in the drawing room when she went down to dinner.

Rebel stripped off her clothes, preparatory to taking a shower. She was about to step into the bathroom when there was a knock on her bedroom door. She quickly slipped her arms into her silk wraparound and called out, "Come in," not even pausing to consider that it might be anyone other than a maid. She walked out of the dressing room, still fastening the tie belt of the flimsy cover-up, and looked up inquiringly to find Hugh Davenport standing just inside her bedroom.

A wave of confusion sent heat flooding through her body. The memory of shared passion throbbed through the tension that leapt between them, making Rebel extremely conscious of her nakedness beneath the thin silk. She nervously fingered the edges of the robe as she waited for him to speak. Her mouth had gone completely dry.

He stared at her with a devouring intensity that sent electric tingles right down to her toes. She had no control whatsoever over the desire that curled through her stomach, that tightened her breasts and drew his eyes to the revealing thrust of her nipples against the clinging silk. Her breathing was reduced to fast, shallow sips of air. Her heart hammered a treacherous plea for some move from him, anything to end this dreadful suspense.

He closed his eyes.

Tight.

It didn't help.

In almost a frenzy of frustration, she watched his face become more and more harshly etched, drawn in sharp lines of painful restraint. When the dark eyes opened again, they begged a thousand tortured questions. Yet when he spoke he didn't address the critical issues between them at all.

"I forgot to tell you, it slipped my mind—there are people coming for dinner tonight, especially to see you, to talk about the orphans who were shipped to Australia."

His brusque words filtered slowly through the chaos of her mind. She worked some much needed moisture into her mouth. "What people?" she asked, finally realising he was not ready to disclose whatever feelings he had about Celeste. Nor had he come with any intention of pursuing the sexual and emotional advantage he had pressed this afternoon. To Rebel it was the worst possible anticlimax, and she could feel herself wilting under its negative impact, wilting and dying a little inside.

"Malcolm Baird and his wife, Roslyn," he replied, each word a flat, deadly trajectory that deliberately defused the explosion of feeling that had simmered on the edge of shattering both his world and hers.

"I told you last night about Malcolm having been here some time ago," he continued quickly, urgently, erratically, not allowing himself time to flirt with temptation again. "Since he knew the orphans had been brought to Davenport Hall, I wondered if he might be able to tell me how to go about finding where they had been before coming here. In case your mother's line could be traced. Relatives found. I thought you might like to do that."

She closed her eyes, almost swaying from the debilitating weakness sweeping through her. Somehow she dredged up the strength to respond. "It was a kind thought, Hugh," she choked out. Her mind sluggishly registered the fact that he had cared, for her sake.

"For a monster," he muttered in savage self-derision.

"Don't!" The protest leapt to her lips. She stepped forward.

His hand jerked up in a warding-off gesture. "Leave it, Rebel!" he commanded, his aristocratic pride returning in full force.

She froze in mid step. She saw his throat move in a convulsive swallow. Then as though it was second nature to him he produced a voice strained of all emotion, polite, polished, cultured by a heritage that went back hundreds of years.

"I contacted Malcolm Baird this morning. He was interested in the fact that the orphans had been shipped to Australia. He wanted to know more about it. He sounded keen to meet you, so I invited him and his wife for dinner. They're quite an elderly couple, but very interesting company. They're due to arrive quite soon, so if you'll excuse me..."

"Of course. Thank you," Rebel managed stiffly.

For a long time she stared at the door that had closed behind him, feeling the chill of rejection creep through her. Because of her, he had been brought to face a reality that burdened him with guilt and shame. He had misjudged and mistreated an innocent child. And he knew that Rebel knew. To him that was intolerable. All the more so because of the attraction between them.

The wretched irony was she had won, yet in winning she had lost her heart's desire. Nothing was ever won without some sacrifice, she reminded herself, but it didn't make her feel any better. This was something she hadn't anticipated, and the blow was all the more devastating because it had caught her unprepared, even looking forward to a reconciliation that might lead to immeasurable happiness. Whereas almost the exact reverse had come about. The truth had driven an irreconcilable wedge between her and Hugh Davenport.

She did not doubt for one moment that Hugh would be more than honourable in fulfilling what should be done for the child, now that he realised how deeply in error he had been. Inevitably there would be ups and downs in the bonding that would gradually evolve. No-one turned over a new leaf without some heart-burn along the way. But the basis of an understanding had been born. That was some comfort for the bleak loneliness in her soul.

Conscious time was passing, Rebel forced herself to go through all the mechanical tasks of getting ready to meet the people who were coming to talk to her. While she showered and dressed, she disciplined herself into blocking out any further thoughts of Hugh and Celeste, and deliberately considered the idea of tracing her mother's family line.

It would be interesting to know where her mother had come from and what had led to her being an orphan. But Rebel was not really drawn to the idea of finding some distant relatives. They would be strangers to her, and she would be a stranger to them. Apart from which, she would never be able to put aside the fact they had not offered to take in and love an orphaned child. To Rebel's mind, nothing excused abandoning a child to an uncertain fate.

Besides, she didn't need any other family than the one she had. Perhaps it was better for her own dark heritage to remain dark. It wasn't really important. She was content with who she was now, and she preferred people to judge her on that, not who her parents were. Celeste was an object lesson on that score.

As she checked her appearance in the full-length mirror in the dressing room, Rebel smiled ruefully at her choice of dress. She was not firing on all cylinders tonight, and she had automatically eschewed bright colours. The soft muted tones of beige and apricot and moss green in the tiny floral print probably reflected her despondent mood.

It was a quiet dress, but very feminine and elegant nonetheless. The graceful flow of the full three-quarter-length sleeves set off the drop waist, which skimmed Rebel's curves to her hips. A low sash drew attention to the unusual gores in the swirling skirt, where tiny rows of frills alternated with sunray pleats. The beige high heels Rebel had slipped onto her feet were completely plain in contrast to the fussy femininity of the skirt.

Satisfied that she was presentable to England's leading historian and his wife, Rebel went downstairs with a fairly confident step, yet her confidence wavered as she reached the doors to the drawing room. It was not only Malcolm and Roslyn Baird she had to face. The evening ahead would inevitably be fraught with the unspoken tensions running between Hugh and herself. But it would be just as bad for him, she told herself, and if he could rise to the occasion, so could she. Polished politeness was not the sole province of earls.

However, Rebel found it very difficult to maintain a resolute composure when she entered the drawing room and saw him. Dressed in a formal black dinner jacket, he looked so devastatingly handsome that her heart contracted with pain. She wrenched her eyes away from him and concentrated fiercely on the guests.

They had both risen to their feet at her entrance. Malcolm Baird had a very distinguished mane of white hair and a distinctly noble face, the kind that one imagined for a Roman senator in ancient times. His wife was also white-haired, but with a tight mass of short curls that framed a face that was still pretty despite her years. Both were formally dressed, he in dinner jacket, she in a moss-green brocade suit.

Roslyn Baird had chosen to wear the same colour as herself, Rebel thought, but instantly brushed the meaningless coincidence aside. It was a popular colour this season.

Malcolm Baird came forward to greet her as Hugh made the introductions. The elderly historian grasped her hand warmly with both of his, and his eyes smiled into hers for far too long. He was taking too much notice of them. Rebel started to move back. She didn't like people looking too closely at her eyes, didn't like any remarks made about their oddity.

But his grasp on her hand tightened, stopping her from moving away. Then, to her further unease, his gaze dropped to her jaw line, tracing quickly along the slight angularity of her bone structure. He took a deep breath and lifted his eyes to hers again. To Rebel's bewilderment they were sheened with moisture.

"My dear child," he said in a throaty burr. "I cannot express the pleasure, the joy I have in this meeting." He retained his hold on her with one hand as he stretched out the other to his wife. "Roslyn..."

The elderly woman seemed unsteady on her feet as she moved forward. She grasped his hand as though she needed his support, and he quickly gathered her in to his side, his arm hugging her tightly to him. The woman looked at Rebel with a yearning hunger that discomfited Rebel further.

"Mrs. Baird," she acknowledged politely, at a loss to know how else to respond to the strangeness of their behaviour.

"There is no doubt now, my love," Malcolm Baird said softly to his wife. "Look at her eyes."

The woman stared at Rebel's eyes. Then her own filled with tears. "Oh, Malcolm!" she choked. "After all these years!"

He cleared his throat and made a valiant effort to contain his emotion. "You must find this very strange, my dear," he said to Rebel. "And I can only beg your forbearance until we can explain it all to you. Perhaps we should sit down first."

Rebel shot a sharply inquiring look at Hugh as they moved to the sofas that flanked the huge fireplace. He returned a dark frown, which didn't reassure her at all. Without asking, he brought her a glass of sherry. Then he moved away, settling himself in an armchair at a distance from her and the Bairds, who sat facing her from the opposite sofa.

It was clear to Rebel he intended to take no part in whatever was about to happen. It made her feel very alone. She looked at the Bairds and fiercely wished they hadn't come.

And what did her eyes have to do with anything? She hated people noticing the irregularity of her eyes. It took away all their mystique. She *liked* to think of it as mystique. And why were they looking at her as though she were the eighth wonder of the world?

Again Malcolm Baird cleared his throat. "I don't know how best to tell you this. It's a long story, and very painful to my wife and myself. Over fifty years ago we lost a daughter, the only child we were ever to have. Despite all our efforts, so many futile searches, it was only very recently the government made documents available under the Freedom of Information Act, and I was able to trace her to Davenport Hall. She was one of a group of orphans who had been sheltered here during the war. But here the trail ended. All further records were destroyed in the war. I could not find out what had happened to the children. Where they were taken from here. My wife and I had given up all hope of ever finding out until Hugh's call this morning."

Rebel felt considerably relieved by this explanation. And sympathetic to the Bairds's plight. To be suddenly handed hope of finding their daughter so late in their lives certainly excused their emotional reaction to her. At least to them she was the bearer of good news.

"Well, I can help you with that, Mr. Baird," Rebel said sympathetically. "All the orphans were shipped to Australia on the HMS *Strathfieldsay.* You could probably find records at that end."

"My dear, we know now that we will never find our daughter," he replied sadly. "She is forever lost to us. Our consolation, if you will allow it to be so, is in finding a granddaughter."

Rebel frowned her bewilderment. "*If* I allow . . . ?"

Her heart stopped dead. The way they were looking at her, the comment about her eyes . . . She shook her head. It was too incredible to accept. Again she shot a sharply inquiring look at Hugh Davenport, but he seemed to be studying the sherry glass in his hands. She looked at the Bairds.

"I don't think I understand you," she said bluntly.

"I realise this must come as a shock to you. A pleasant shock, we hope," Malcolm Baird said anxiously, squeezing his wife's hand. "Hugh told me that your mother's name was Valerie Griffith, and that you'd come to Davenport Hall in the hope of finding out something of her life. I came here some time ago for the same reason. You see, my dear, Valerie Griffith was our daughter. And you—there can be no doubt now. There are distinctive family features that confirm it beyond doubt. You are our granddaughter."

Rebel stared at him, noticing for the first time that the shape of his jaw was similar to hers, although it was blurred by the fleshiness of age. But his eyes were brown. His wife's... Rebel felt a sickening recoil in her heart as she saw that Roslyn Baird's eyes were hazel and held the same tantalising shift of colour as her own.

They were her grandparents!

Her mother's parents!

Alive, well-to-do people who had no business losing a little child! Rebel's sympathy for them was crushed under the memory of her mother's plight.

"How could you lose a daughter?" she demanded. "How could you let her go? My mother... my mother..."

A huge lump blocked her throat. She leapt to her feet, too disturbed to keep looking at these people who could have given her mother a rich, secure life. And didn't! She walked blindly away from them, not thinking of where she was going, only knowing she didn't want to look at them any more.

Hugh stepped in front of her, bringing her to a halt. She glared at him belligerently, hating him for having arranged this meeting, hating him for denying both of them what could have been between them, hating his pride, hating his English affinity to these English people who had denied her mother.

The reasonable part of her mind told her she was being unreasonable. He had invited the Bairds here as a kindness to her. But she didn't want it. Her mother had given birth to her alone, raised her alone, died alone. And Rebel didn't want to know these people who should have been there. Who should have loved their daughter and supported her and been there for her!

The dark eyes met hers unflinchingly. Slowly and steadily they bored through the turbulence of her emotions. He lifted a hand and very deliberately laid his palm on her cheek.

"Give them a chance, Rebel," he said in a low, raw voice. "I know it hurts. I know you don't want to listen to them or try to understand them. But you could be wrong to turn away and reject them. Very wrong. And if you are..."

He was echoing her words to him about Celeste, challenging her to do what she had demanded of him, telling her he knew what she felt because he had felt the same about Christine's child.

"They don't have many years left, Rebel," he added more forcefully. "Give them a chance."

You won't give me one, she wanted to retort. Her eyes warred bitterly with his for several seconds, accusing him of hypocrisy.

"At least listen to what they have to say," he rasped. "You pride yourself on being fair, don't you? So show me you practise what you preach, Rebel."

"One rule for you, and another for me, my lord?" she mocked.

"Do you want to be a monster?" he countered harshly.

"Unfortunately, I'm all too human."

"And open to error."

"You, too," she reminded him tersely.

"I, too," he agreed, not flinching from his judicial stance.

"Fine! I'll give them a chance!" she snapped. "I just hope my mother doesn't turn in her grave."

CHAPTER NINE

HUGH WAS RIGHT.

Just as she had been right about Celeste.

Malcolm and Roslyn had been students at Oxford together. She was from a well-educated middle-class family. He from the upper class, both too young to legally marry without parental consent. His family had opposed the relationship. Roslyn had been made to feel like a social outcast when Malcolm had presented her to them. One pressure after another had been callously applied to make them part.

Both Roslyn and Malcolm fought against the edict never to see each other again. The liaison continued. A child was conceived. They were both still under the legal age of consent, which at that time was twenty-one. They were forbidden to marry and Roslyn was taken away, hidden from him, their child forcibly taken from her and put out for adoption. Apparently they did those kinds of things in those days. Malcolm never spoke to his father again from that time onwards.

Then came the war. Malcolm had been a guards officer on leave in London, and he had caught sight of Roslyn getting off a bus. Having found her, Malcolm swore they would never be parted by anyone again, and they were married by special license. He vowed to find their lost child and get her back.

His transfer to Montgomery's staff in the western desert enforced a postponement of that quest. After Egypt came Italy, Normandy and finally Berlin. When the war was over, every inquiry he made about the child, every search led only to a dead end.

The sorrow of having lost their child was all the more poignant when they found they were unable to have any more children. Neither of them could ever forget the daughter who had been taken from them. When Malcolm had found the reference pertaining to the sheltering of orphans at Davenport Hall, he had come and discovered their daughter's name on the list. It was all the more shattering when he could find no record of where the children had been taken from here.

Rebel felt deeply ashamed of her hasty judgment. These people had suffered far longer than her mother had, and were victims of their respective families, just as Celeste had been. She tried to make up for her earlier rejection of them by telling them all she could remember of her mother.

Then, over dinner, at Hugh's deft prompting, she told them of her life with the James family, deliberately glossing over the painful period of time between her mother's death and her adoption. It seemed to lift their spirits to hear how happy she had been with her adopted family, and how she had set out to make a career for herself and succeeded.

They looked at her with pride. Possessive pride. And somehow that did not sit well with Rebel. They had nothing to do with her life. They were still strangers to her, and although she was sorry for them, she felt no sense of belonging at all.

It made her reconsider how Hugh must feel about Celeste. He did not believe the little girl belonged to him, not in any blood-relation sense. He had been made legally responsible for her, much against his inclination. He might feel sorry for the child now, but love—even affection—could not be generated in the space of a few hours. It took time for negative feelings to change to something positive.

It was an emotionally draining evening, and Rebel felt a somewhat guilty surge of relief when it came to an end. The Bairds gave her their London address and pressed her to come and visit them, stay with them if she would, whenever it was convenient to her. They were not demanding, but Rebel was intensely conscious of their need. They wanted her to fill the tragic gap in their lives, and she wasn't sure she could. Not entirely, anyway. But she would certainly go out of her way to keep in contact with them for the rest of their lives. What she desperately needed was a breathing space to think about it all.

Hugh escorted them out to their car. For a man who had just been through a traumatic experience, he had certainly risen above it tonight. He had sat back and been discreetly unintrusive for the most part, but he had demonstrated a keen awareness of the feelings of his guests at a number of critical moments. The consummate host, Rebel thought ruefully, wishing she had been able to match his impeccable manners.

Ashamed that she hadn't handled the situation with more sensitivity, Rebel headed upstairs before Hugh returned from seeing the Bairds on their way. As tired as she was, Rebel knew sleep would be a long time coming tonight. Too much had happened today, too much that weighed on her mind and heart and soul. Her feet automatically turned to the flight of stairs that took her to the second floor.

As she entered the schoolroom, Rebel was once more assailed by the sense of timelessness, as though all the years melded, losing any individual form or meaning. Somehow the effect was even stronger tonight, perhaps because of the soft shadows thrown by the fading English twilight. A strange sort of peace seeped into her as she walked slowly around the room, touching the desks, the easel with its old-fashioned blackboard, the rocking horse, which tipped into smooth action despite its age. She slid off her shoes, curled up on one of the window seats and leant her head against a pane of glass, looking out, looking down.

Below her stretched the ancient avenue of elms, leading to the stone gateway where she had stood—when? Three days ago? Several lifetimes ago? Celeste's life would be different now. Perhaps Hugh's, as well. As for herself, her mother had drawn her here, and here to this place had come her mother's parents. A fifty-year cycle of loneliness and misery closed.

Tears gathered in her eyes and trickled down her cheeks as she thought of the love that had been there for her mother, half a world away, if only it could have been reached. It was there for Rebel now. She was the focal link between the parents who had been robbed of being parents and the daughter who had been robbed of what was rightly hers from birth.

Was this what it had all been about, the tug on her soul that had insisted she stay at Davenport Hall? Was it finished now? Or was there more?

Rebel desperately wanted more.

The sound of the door opening jerked her head away from the windowpane. The room was almost dark, but neither she nor Hugh needed any artificial light to see each other.

"I thought you might be here," he said softly.

Rebel's heart pounded too painfully for her to think of any reply. It was almost as if her need for him had conjured him up. He did not switch on any lights, and as he moved slowly towards her she felt an aching yearning to always have him with her.

He sat at the other end of the window seat. His face was in shadow but it was turned her way. "I want you to know that I was unaware of any relationship between the Bairds and your mother," he said quietly. "Malcolm gave me no prior hint of it. I had no idea of what was to happen, Rebel, and I'm sorry that I was so preoccupied with my own thoughts that I failed to pick up signals that should have warned me there was more to the meeting than I had anticipated."

"You have nothing to apologise for, Hugh."

He shook his head. "You were thrown into shock. You needed time. And I was harsh with you."

"A good slap in the face has been known to bring people out of shock," she commented dryly.

"If it had been done for that reason, I could congratulate myself. But the truth of the matter is I was retaliating. And that's not something I'm proud of."

The regret, the awkward humility in his voice made Rebel forget her raw feelings for a moment.

"It doesn't matter, Hugh," she said softly. "It worked. And I was wrong to act as I did. I'm grateful to you for making me face up to practising what I preach. Otherwise..." She heaved a deep sigh to relieve the tightness in her chest.

"You would have come round, Rebel. It's not in you to turn your back on people."

She shook her head. "I don't know. I thought I knew myself, but nothing seems clear any more."

"It was very clear to me that you carefully withheld a great deal that might have hurt Malcolm and Roslyn tonight. You have nothing to reproach yourself for, Rebel. You dealt very kindly with them." He paused then gently added, "If there's anything I can do for you..."

Rebel closed her eyes, even though it was too dark for him to see into them. There was so much he could do for her, but she couldn't ask. It had to come from him. Because he wanted it as much as she did.

"I guess I'll sort it all out sooner or later," she said flatly.

Her ears ached, listening for him to stand up, to leave her. Her whole body was tensely attuned to any shift from him. The silence stretched on. He didn't move. And finally he spoke again, his voice very low and strained.

"That deal we made, Rebel..."

Her heart plummeted. He was going to ask her to leave. And why not? Her job here was done. Or at least the right direction had been pointed out and accepted. She could not have achieved much more anyway.

"I was wondering, if it wasn't too much trouble for you, and if you can overlook my—the way I acted and what I asked of you this afternoon, which I assure you will not be repeated..." She heard him drag in a deep breath and slowly expel it. "Would you consider staying on with us beyond the week we agreed upon?"

Rebel's eyes flew open in sheer surprise. Her pulse kicked into overtime. "You want me to stay, Hugh?" she whispered, unable to find more voice.

"Yes." The quick reply had a very positive punch, yet almost in the same breath, he added, "I do realise you might feel the Bairds have more claim on your time. And of course you must do what you feel is right. But I would do all I can to accommodate whatever you wanted. Invite your grandparents here as guests if you'd like that."

He really did want her to stay. That was very clear. But his reasons for wanting it were left unstated, and Rebel had a sinking feeling they all centred on Celeste.

She took a deep breath and attacked the issue head-on. "You can't just leave Celeste to me, Hugh. I'll stay for a while, but not as a minder who frees you of responsibility. It has to start being a three-way thing, or Celeste will feel all the more lost when I go. That's when you'll have to be there for her, in a very solid capacity. The longer I stay, the greater her need will be for you to make up for my leaving."

"I'll work with you as best I can, Rebel," he promised gravely.

"And I'll help as much as I can," she promised in return. "I do appreciate how hard it is for you, Hugh. The way you feel about her..."

"No. It won't be so hard."

He heaved a deep sigh and stood up. Again Rebel thought he meant to leave her, having made the apologies he had felt constrained to make and secured her agreement to stay and help with Celeste. Disappointment dragged at her heart. For a little while they had seemed so close in the darkness.

But again she was wrong. He did not leave. He walked over to one of the school desks. His fingers traced over the old scars on its lid, just as hers had done last night.

"This was Geoffrey's desk," he said, his tone one of sad reminiscence. "We were very close as children. He was only eighteen months older than I. He loved games, animals, laughter..."

Rebel held her tongue, sensing his need to unburden himself of things that had weighed too long and too heavily on his mind and heart. It was easier to do that in the darkness, and perhaps this was the time, the place, and she was the person, someone who was apart from the life he had known, yet intimately connected to this moment.

"Tonight I agreed to let Celeste have a dog of her own. And the look on her face... For the first time I saw a flash of my brother in her. It's possible—Christine lied about everything, but it is possible that Celeste is Geoffrey's child and all that's left of him. When I held her in my arms..."

He shook his head and when he spoke again his voice was furred with emotion. "I will make it all up to her, Rebel. It won't be so hard."

Rebel's mind raced with excitement. If Hugh felt like that, there would be no problem with Celeste. So why did he want her to stay? Was it only for an easing through an initial awkwardness with his niece, or was there a far more personal reason behind his request that she stay on at Davenport Hall?

We can have something... That was what he had said—and felt—this afternoon. Whatever he was thinking and feeling now, he wanted more time with her. That gave her cause for hope, didn't it?

He turned around and propped himself on the desktop. "I haven't thanked you for all you've done for Celeste so far. She seems to have taken everything you've said to her very much to heart."

There was a question in his voice, and Rebel answered it because it was important for him to know. "That's mostly because I listen to her, Hugh, and give her replies that she can relate to. Authoritarian proclamations will only ever stir rebellion in Celeste. She's a very intelligent little girl. Give her a lead, and a reason for it, and she can work a lot out for herself. That gives her a sense of pride in her own achievement. Makes her feel happy inside. I think you could have a very rewarding relationship with her. In time. And with care."

There was a long silence.

Rebel sensed a withdrawal into himself, a need for self-examination, reappraisal. When he eventually spoke again, it was in a tone of self-disgust. "You were right to call me a monster."

"No, Hugh," she said quietly. "A monster wouldn't have tried."

He made a harsh, contemptuous sound and pushed away from the desk. He paced around the schoolroom as though driven by inner demons. "I didn't try for Celeste. I did it for you. I wanted you. And if that was what I had to do to get you..." He paused, and the savagery in his voice deepened. "You see what kind of man I am?"

He made a derisive click of his fingers. "So much for any sense of right or honour! I didn't care about what was best for you any more. And I refused to believe any part of what you said about Celeste. My only thought was that Christine was not going to stop me from having what I wanted. My conscience..."

He gave a wild mocking laugh. "Oh, I did a good job of killing that! Stone dead! I smothered it with so many justifications..."

He stopped pacing. "But then you'd have to know about Christine to understand that. Beautiful angelic sexy Christine! With a heart as black as the ace of spades!" he said bitterly.

Rebel wanted to know. Christine was the key to all the darkness at Davenport Hall. Yet Rebel was conscious of being an outsider who had no right to know, so she didn't ask. She maintained a sympathetic silence, fiercely hoping that Hugh would spill it all out to her.

The revelation of his motive for trying with Celeste did not shock her at all. To the contrary, it stirred an almost exultant satisfaction. If the strength of his desire for her had driven him so far, maybe his feelings ran as deeply as her own. Surely there was a chance, if only the lingering darkness of Christine could be dispelled.

He started walking around the room again, restlessly picking things up and putting them down. "I curse the day I brought her here," he said savagely. "I was so besotted with her, so blindly infatuated, that I couldn't wait to present her to my family—this ultimate prize of womanhood! I had no idea that Christine had another prize in mind. That nothing was going to stop her from becoming the Countess of Stanthorpe."

He stared at a rag clown he had picked up from one of the shelves. "She had my brother bewitched in no time flat. Only too ready to marry her when she announced she was pregnant by him. But once he was hooked and the title secured, her halo started slipping within weeks of the marriage. She made Geoffrey's life a hell on earth. It twisted him into an entirely different person."

He slowly repositioned the rag clown on the shelf. "I don't believe his death was an accident. He'd been warned the skiing slope was dangerous. I think he just didn't care any more, soaring down a clean expanse of white snow in a final game with fate. I wonder if he knew what Christine would do."

"What did she do?" Rebel prompted softly as he seemed about to sink into a dark, brooding reverie.

Hugh threw her a derisive look. "The sorrowing widow returned to Davenport Hall," he continued, his voice dipped in acid. "The only problem was she no longer had a right to occupy it. But Christine already had a solution worked out."

He gave a mirthless little laugh and started pacing again, tossing his words at Rebel in bitter bursts. "On the day of my brother's funeral, only hours after Geoffrey had been laid to rest, she came to my bedroom to tell me that her marriage to Geoffrey had been a terrible mistake. She had been seduced by the idea of being a countess and bitterly regretted it because she had truly loved me and still did. She tried to show me how much she still loved me and wanted me."

His breath hissed out in sheer loathing and disgust. "I dragged her kicking and screaming down the stairs and out to her black Porsche. I threw her into the car and told her to go to hell or wherever else she liked. She was never to darken the doors of Davenport Hall again."

All the violent emotions he had felt that night seemed to swirl around the schoolroom. Then, as if they had been exorcised, a sense of quiet finality gradually took over.

"The coroner thought it was probably grief that caused her to drive at such speed on the motorway," Hugh said heavily. "I could have told him it was blind, vicious rage. Christine was probably still mouthing obscenities when she crashed. But the dead can't give evidence. And I was content for everything she was to die with her."

But it hadn't died with her, Rebel thought. And Hugh had not rested content. He had been left with Christine's child, and his hatred for the mother had made a monster of Celeste. Even as the thought passed through Rebel's mind, Hugh roused himself out of the past and into the present.

"I've been as blind about Celeste as I once was about Christine," he said regretfully. "Every time I looked at that small, angelic face I saw a reincarnation of her mother. That, added to her destructive behaviour..."

He sighed and shook his head as though trying to shake off the madness that had possessed him. His voice dropped to a raw gravel. "But when she looked at me tonight, it wasn't Christine. It was Geoffrey. And all you'd said to me in the study rushed through my mind like an army of hornets, attacking all I'd ever thought about the child. And that was when..."

"When you really tried," Rebel softly inserted.

"Yes," came the bleak admission.

"It doesn't matter how or why or when, Hugh. The only important thing is that you didn't fail her when she reached out to you."

There were several long tense moments before he asked, "You can dismiss everything else like that, Rebel?"

His honesty demanded an equal honesty from her. "I wish Christine's influence had died with her. That's what I've been fighting ever since I got here. Both with you and Celeste. If you can now put it behind you, Hugh, then the battle is more than half won with Celeste."

She took a deep breath, aware she was about to tread dangerous ground. "I didn't plan what happened between us in your office this afternoon," she said quietly. "But if it accomplished what all the reasoning in the world couldn't, believe me, I would have planned it if I could have anticipated such a result. As far as I'm concerned, all's well that ends well."

He gave a rueful little laugh. "You are one hell of a sales person, Rebel Griffith James. I wish I could exonerate myself of all my crimes as easily as that."

"What's done is done, Hugh," she said quietly. "It's what you do from here on that counts. My parents used to say, 'Tomorrow is always the first day of the rest of your life. What you make of it is up to you.' It invariably pushed us into positive thinking."

"The first day of the rest of my life," he repeated softly, musingly.

In the silence that followed, Rebel felt a growing lift in the atmosphere, a settling of peace. She had a fancy that the ancient stones of Davenport Hall breathed a sigh of relief as the darkness of Christine finally took leave of them.

Her heart gave an excited leap when Hugh stepped towards her. He walked slowly to the window seat, bent to pick up her shoes, then sat down and drew her stockinged feet onto his lap. Rebel was so startled by this action that she sat mesmerised as his fingers stroked softly along her toes and trailed up to her finely boned ankles.

"One doesn't really think of angels as having human feet," he said in teasing whimsy.

"Angels?" Rebel croaked huskily. Little quivers of excitement were running up her legs.

"I'm not quite sure which one you are. The Avenging Angel or the Angel of Mercy," he mused, slipping her shoes onto her feet.

A self-conscious laugh gurgled from Rebel's throat. "I assure you I'm alarmingly human." It *was* alarming, the way his touch was playing havoc with all her nerve endings.

He stood up, took her hands and drew her off the window seat. Rebel felt so shaky she could barely stand. "I am rather counting on that," he said in his velvet voice. Which shook her even more.

If he had taken her in his arms then, if he had kissed her, if he had wanted to make love to her, Rebel doubted she would have been capable of turning away from him—right or wrong. But he didn't do any of those things.

He released one of her hands. He took a more possessive grip on the other and drew her along with him as he started towards the schoolroom door. "I think it's time to put an end to today," he said decisively. Then in a softer tone he added, "To sleep, perchance to dream . . ."

Rebel suddenly felt very tired. Bed did seem like a good idea now. Tomorrow would be a new beginning at Davenport Hall. A new beginning perhaps for lots of things.

There was a warm friendliness, an unspoken companionship or even partnership in the firm clasp of Hugh's hand as they walked downstairs together. The distant reserve of chilly or aristocratic politeness seemed to have been put to rest along with Christine and the painful past. Rebel hoped it would never come back. But the other hope she had been nursing was quivering uncertainly over what this change of manner meant.

Hugh accompanied her to her bedroom door, opened it for her, then turned to face her, a slight smile on his lips and a teasing warmth in his eyes. "I've been taught quite a few lessons today," he said. "If I can quote Celeste correctly... Rebel said you should hug and kiss goodnight, so you can forget all the bad things that have happened before you go to sleep."

He lifted her hands to his shoulders. "You have to put your arms around my neck, and then I hold you tight." His arms slid around her waist and pressed her so close to him that Rebel dizzily wondered if it was his heart she felt beating, or her own, or both in a mad pounding unison.

"And then I rub my cheek over your hair like this..."

But it was not done with the soothing tenderness of an adult with a child. His cheek swept over her hair once, but his mouth burned a trail of kisses back, kisses that tilted her head up to his, that swept her curls away from her forehead, that pressed her eyes closed, that caressed the tip of her nose, that brushed her lips with a slow, tantalising sensuality, feather-light pressures that tingled deliciously, that explored the shape of her mouth from every angle, that gradually seduced her lips apart.

There was no driving passion in the deepening of his kiss, yet somehow the gentler, more exploratory invasion was even more intimate than any passionate demand. A melting sweetness coursed through Rebel's whole body. She was totally immersed in delicious sensations, and a little moan of protest choked from her throat when he withdrew. Almost instantly his lips brushed hers again, lingering for several moments before reluctantly lifting away.

"Goodnight. And thank you. For the miracle," he murmured, dropping a last kiss on her forehead. Then he gently extracted himself from her embrace, ushered her into the bedroom and firmly closed the door between them.

CHAPTER TEN

REBEL DIDN'T KNOW what to think. Had it only been a thank-you kiss? Did it mean more? Surely Hugh wouldn't have been so—so thorough about it just to say thank you. Yet he hadn't tried to push it any further, and he certainly hadn't been in the grip of passionate desire.

I'll know better tomorrow, Rebel assured herself as she got ready for bed. Everything should be a lot clearer tomorrow. She simply had to sleep on it. That was all. Besides, in her heart of hearts, she did not want a sexual relationship with Hugh Davenport. Not if that was where it stopped.

Rebel slept late the next morning. When she came down to breakfast, both Hugh and Celeste were at the table. The moment she entered the room their eyes fastened on her, and their faces were lit by smiles that seemed to reflect the sunshine streaming through the long windows.

No darkness.

Not even a lingering trace of it.

Rebel's spirits soared.

"Good morning," she said, her inner joy lilting through her voice and spreading into her answering smile.

Hugh returned the greeting in a warm, welcoming tone that lifted Rebel's spirits even higher. He looked very much the English country squire this morning in a forest-green turtleneck and tweed jacket. The thought came to her that it wouldn't matter what he wore, he carried an ingrained air of breeding that automatically commanded admiration. Which accounted for her quickened pulse, but didn't quite account for the shaky weakness in her legs.

Celeste leapt off her chair and skipped over to Rebel in a burst of uncontainable excitement. "I'm getting a dog," she cried.

Rebel instinctively scooped the child up in her arms. "Hey! That's great news!"

There was no wriggling protest from Celeste. She perched quite happily at eye level with Rebel and bubbled on. "Uncle Hugh rang Sir Roger Woolcott this morning, 'cause he's a judge at dog shows and knows all the best breeding kennels. And I'm going to get a Yorkshire terrier. A little pup. Only six weeks old. Uncle Hugh said I can choose it myself, and we're going to look at them after breakfast."

"What an exciting morning you're going to have!"

"Yes!" The big blue eyes were sparkling with happy anticipation. "Can you come with us, Rebel? You don't have to go to work, do you? You haven't got work clothes on."

Which was true enough. The blue jeans and cherry-red sweater were not her professional clothes, but she did have work to do. However, Celeste didn't wait for a reply. She swivelled to face her uncle. "Rebel can come with us, can't she, Uncle Hugh?" she asked eagerly.

He had stood to hold out Rebel's chair for her, and the dark eyes shot her a look of warm satisfaction as he replied, "Of course. You're very welcome, Rebel. But I think we'd better let her eat first, Celeste."

The child laughed and slithered out of Rebel's hold. She grabbed Rebel's hand and hauled her towards the chair Hugh was holding. "Come on. We're almost finished. I wanted to wake you up but Uncle Hugh said you needed a good sleep 'cause there were people here last night who kept you up late."

Rebel flashed Hugh a searching look as she sat down. The dark eyes returned a glint of secret intimacy that squeezed Rebel's heart and sent a rush of tingling warmth around her bloodstream. Fortunately she had time to recover some composure while Hugh and Celeste resumed their places at the table, but the sense of togetherness was like a wild intoxicant in her mind.

Celeste's big blue eyes beamed exultant delight at her. "I tried what you said, Rebel, and Uncle Hugh did listen."

"Yes. And I'm quite a fast learner, as well," Hugh said, his lips twitching in amusement.

"So am I, Uncle Hugh," Celeste said smugly.

Rebel felt caught between laughter and tears, and completely choked up. Everything was working so well this morning. It was as though Hugh's chilly authority and Celeste's mutinous defiance had melted away overnight. If this was the reward for the battle she had fought, Rebel was well content. At least, that was what she told herself. But she knew it was a lie. There was no contentment in her mind at all. Nor in her body.

The maid came in to take her order for breakfast and Rebel settled on tea and toast, too full of emotion to have any appetite for food. Even the maid smiled, infected by the unusually happy atmosphere.

We're like a family, Rebel thought, then sternly told herself she was getting a bit too fanciful, and the magic of this moment might very well be only that—temporary magic, not permanent. It was madness to indulge in such a fantasy, madness to feed it.

A goodnight kiss—a thank-you kiss—need not mean anything more than that. It behove her to set the ground for the future relationship between Hugh and his niece, not grab for her own self-gratification. She was not part of Hugh's and Celeste's life. Not really. If she didn't keep remembering that, she could get herself in deep trouble. This sense of family intimacy was dangerous.

"Thank you for inviting me to accompany you this morning," she forced herself to say. "But don't let me hold you up. I don't have to go to London, but I do have a lot of paperwork to do, and telephone calls to make. So if I get through all my business this morning while you and your uncle choose your pup, Celeste, I'll be free to enjoy myself with you when you come home."

The child's face fell a little then brightened again when Rebel added, "We could take the pup for a walk about the grounds and show it its new home."

Celeste instantly turned to her uncle. "We'll have to get a leash, Uncle Hugh. I don't want my dog running away and getting lost."

"We'll get a leash, and a bed basket, and everything else that a dog needs, Celeste," he assured her. "Now, if we're not to wait for Rebel, why don't you go and find Mrs. Tomkins and warn her we're bringing a dog home so she can order the right food for it?"

Celeste was off like a shot.

Hugh turned to Rebel with a rueful smile. "Why do I get the feeling that I've just been thrown to the wolves?"

Rebel stuck grimly to firm common sense. "Why share the glory? It's your initiative. You should make the most of the returns."

His eyebrows slanted a reproof. "What if I need a helping hand?"

She raised her eyebrows in mock surprise. "With two fast learners like you and Celeste, how can you go wrong?"

He laughed, the dark eyes caressing her with sparkling pleasure.

Rebel's stomach curled. It was at that moment that all her feelings about this man merged into a lightning bolt of realisation. She loved him. She wanted to share the rest of her life with him. He was the one she had been waiting for, the one who would be her partner in all things, the father of her children, the head of her family, the man who would always hold her heart.

His laughter turned into a quizzical frown. "Is something wrong, Rebel?"

She snapped out of her daze and forced a smile. "No. Not at all. I was just thinking how nice you look when you laugh."

Nice! her mind mocked. Such an absurd lukewarm word! Hugh was the most riveting man in the world when he laughed.

"I must remember to do it more often," he remarked teasingly, then immediately turned serious. "Rebel, those sponsorships I lined up for you yesterday...there are no strings attached to them. I want you to take them up. If only as a token of my gratitude for the time you're giving us. That's acceptable, isn't it?" he pressed as he saw her recoil from the offer.

"I've always done my own spadework, Hugh. I guess it's a matter of pride," she said quietly. "I'm just not comfortable with patronage."

The dark eyes bored into hers with purposeful intensity. "Nor am I comfortable with taking and not giving."

Pride clashed with pride and created a tension that had nothing to do with business. This was deeply personal, striking at the very roots of their characters— Rebel's self-made independence, the Earl of Stanthorpe's heritage of distributing favours, not taking them.

Celeste came pelting into the room, glowing with excitement. "I told Mrs. Tomkins, Uncle Hugh. Could we go now?"

"Yes," he agreed, and rose from his chair. He gave Rebel one last searing look. "Please consider it. The papers are still on my office desk if you want to look at them.''

"All right," she conceded reluctantly, then turned to smile at Celeste and wish her all the best in choosing a pup.

Rebel spent the next two hours in her room, getting her paperwork up to date and making the necessary calls. It was difficult to concentrate on the business at hand. Hugh's idea of sponsorships from the great chateaux of the wine industry was a good one, but somehow it still felt uncomfortably like a pay-off. He was grateful to her. Grateful. The word was like a pound of doom inside Rebel's head.

Eventually she decided she should go down to the office and at least look. She didn't like accepting the arrangements he had made, yet it was probably ungracious not to. And it would please him if she did.

Mrs. Tomkins met her on the stairs. "Oh, there you are, Miss James! Miss Lumleigh asked to see you. Brooks has put her in the drawing room."

Rebel frowned. "Miss Lumleigh? To see me?"

Mrs. Tomkins gave her a dry little smile. "I understand Sir Roger Woolcott advised Lord Davenport on buying a dog this morning. Miss Lumleigh has brought over a book on the care and characteristics of Yorkshire terriers."

"Oh! You mean she's really waiting for Lord Davenport's return," Rebel interpreted.

"I would think so, Miss James."

Rebel grimaced. The last person Celeste would want to see was Cynthia Lumleigh. In that feeling, Rebel heartily concurred. However, if the snaky blonde was intent on seeing Hugh—which was a dead certainty—Rebel couldn't see how to get rid of her. She briefly and rather bitchily wondered if new pups were ever indiscreet in people's laps.

"I could say you've gone for a walk somewhere," the housekeeper said with unexpected sympathy.

Rebel heaved a resigned sigh. "Thank you, Mrs. Tomkins, but I'd better see her."

The housekeeper also sighed. "I do hope Lady Celeste... I'm afraid that Miss Lumleigh does not bring out the best in her," she said with gross understatement, then beamed approval at Rebel. "Not like you, Miss James. The whole staff has remarked how nice it was to see Lady Celeste so happy this morning. Just like a normal child. A miracle, Brooks declared. A blooming miracle. And, of course, we all know it's your doing."

"Why, thank you, Mrs. Tomkins," Rebel replied warmly, somewhat surprised by this accolade from the household staff.

"I've always believed in giving credit where credit's due. Though I don't think the television documentary had it right about Australians. We've yet to see you being tough at all, Miss James."

Rebel had to laugh. "Oh, I'm fairly tough in a fight, Mrs. Tomkins. Which reminds me. Miss Lumleigh is waiting."

"In the drawing room, Miss James," the housekeeper agreed with a little nod of approval.

Rebel was left with the very strong impression that Cynthia Lumleigh had not won any popularity polls amongst the staff at Davenport Hall. Surely Hugh wouldn't ever seriously consider marrying *her*. He couldn't, Rebel decided grimly. Besides, he wasn't really that cynical. Was he?

All the same, Rebel suffered a painful twinge of uncertainty when she entered the drawing room and found Cynthia Lumleigh stroking a bronze figurine with a proprietarial air. The elegant blonde looked very much at home in these rich surroundings. Born to it, Rebel conceded glumly.

She was very much dressed for the part, as well. The lavender and white silk dress was both stately and feminine. The pearl studs in her ears and the double strand around her long, graceful neck were a nicely discreet show of good jewellery. The lavender strips across the toes of her white shoes were the ultimate touch of class. Her make-up was perfect, and she might have just walked away from the hairdresser. The look of amused condescension in the cold blue eyes that surveyed Rebel's appearance made Rebel feel like a tatty mess.

She stiffened her spine.

All that glitters is not gold, Rebel recited to herself, and Cynthia Lumleigh was pure dross as far as she was concerned. If Hugh couldn't see that, he deserved a fate worse than death!

Cynthia immediately assumed the role of hostess, inviting Rebel to sit with her at the far end of the drawing room where the windows looked out to the ornamental lake. After a spate of polite and totally insincere small talk, which Rebel matched word for word, the snaky blonde finally came to the point of the exercise, leading into it with sweet venom.

"I think Hugh is taking a dreadful risk giving Celeste a dog. The poor little pup will probably be tortured to death."

"More likely loved to death," Rebel corrected her.

A tinkled laugh that gently mocked. "You don't understand, Miss James. Celeste is Christine's child. But then you don't know about Christine, do you?"

Cynthia didn't wait for a reply. Her blue eyes were as hard as bullets as she shot out her lethal brand of poison. "Hugh was totally infatuated with Christine before she married his brother. She was an extremely beautiful woman. A model. A very ambitious model. You would never have believed she had dragged herself up from the slums of Liverpool. But underneath her polished veneer she had a gutter mentality. The most vicious and cruel woman I've ever met. Celeste takes after her mother, not only in looks but in character, as well." She smiled. "But perhaps you understand that kind of character. Having come from a deprived background yourself."

Rebel's hackles rose. "I don't consider myself deprived at all, Miss Lumleigh. In fact, I consider myself more fortunate than most."

The blonde gave her another patronising smile. "Of course. Such an interesting melting pot, your adopted family! I merely meant that, well . . ." She waved an elegant hand. "There's no telling who or what your father was. You said so yourself. And your poor mother, deserted like that, and obviously no family to turn to or you wouldn't have been adopted. And breeding is so important when it comes to a question of marriage."

"It might be to you, Miss Lumleigh. It isn't to me," Rebel stated flatly.

Again the tinkled laugh. "I was forgetting you were Australian. I don't suppose anyone in Australia wants to look too closely at family lines, since the country was settled by convicts. Much more practical just to take people at face value. But I doubt that someone like Hugh thinks like that. Particularly after his experience with Christine."

She paused, sharpening her fangs for the next strike. Rebel said nothing. To a woman as prejudiced and narrow-minded as Cynthia Lumleigh, there was no point in arguing that Australia was the land of the free, a quality that was valued highly by the people who had fled there from repressive class systems and societies. Besides, that really wasn't the point at issue. And what Cynthia had said about Hugh's thinking was more or less what he had implied himself. Rebel couldn't say she didn't care about that. She did care. Very deeply.

Cynthia resumed the attack. "Here in England it's been proven over and over again that expectations are better fulfilled within one's own class. It's a matter of ingrained standards. An acceptable pattern of behaviour. Christine fell far short of it, I'm afraid. But then she was born and bred a commoner. And having witnessed his brother's disastrous marriage, Hugh is hardly likely to make the same mistake, however attractive he might find you, Miss James.''

The deadly blue eyes flitted over Rebel's voluptuously curved figure with an expression of disdainful contempt. ''Sex appeal isn't everything,'' she declared. ''Christine was far sexier than you with her blend of angelic innocence and earthy sensuality. But most men are susceptible to the obvious. After they've had it . . . Well, sex is never lasting, is it? It's simply a *common* denominator between men and women.''

Rebel could feel her face tightening and could do nothing about it. She saw the malicious satisfaction in the super bitch's blue eyes and hated her for it, yet she could not deny that sex was all Hugh had wanted from her yesterday when he had pressed her to come away with him. He had wanted her then, wanted her to be his mistress until he tired of her. He might very well have asked her to stay on at Davenport Hall because he still wanted her in his bed. At some convenient time to him. Perhaps he would suggest coming to Paris with her to clinch the sponsorships. Was that why he was pressing them on her?

Cynthia's smile was dipped in acid indulgence. ''I feel it's only kind to tell you you're wasting your time here at Davenport Hall. After all, when it comes right down to it, you are very common, Miss James.''

''On the contrary,'' a hard voice said. ''Rebel is extraordinarily *uncommon,* Cynthia.''

The blonde's languidly confident pose stiffened as her head whipped around to face the man who had spoken. Rebel did not move. She didn't want to look at Hugh. There was a sick despair in her soul that she didn't want him to see.

"In fact," he continued, his tone biting with icy contempt, "her quality shines above all the women I have ever met. And I count myself very honoured and fortunate that she has consented to be my guest at Davenport Hall."

Cynthia started up from her chair, speaking quickly in urgent appeasement. "Hugh, I was only trying to explain to her—"

"I heard what you were trying to explain, Cynthia," he cut in. "And I'll thank you never to speak for me again. Because your standards are not mine. And never will be. But before you practise your indiscretions elsewhere, let me inform you that Rebel's maternal grandfather is Malcolm Baird, who would have been the fifteenth Earl of Alisdair had he not renounced the title."

"But—but how..." Cynthia spluttered.

"Very simple. Rebel's mother was Malcolm's daughter. And Rebel's heritage goes directly back to the Stuart kings of Scotland. Not that she cares about that. And neither do I. But be very careful what you say about Rebel in future, Cynthia, because I make a very bad and relentless enemy."

Cynthia rounded on Rebel. "Why didn't you say?" she demanded.

"Because it didn't matter to her, Cynthia," Hugh rasped in mounting rage. "And you have outstayed your welcome here."

"Hugh!" The blonde turned a shocked face to him.

"Please leave us now!" he commanded.

"But—"

"Now!"

There was so much explosive violence in the repeated command that not even Cynthia had the hide to risk a further protest. She shot one last venomous look at Rebel, then tossed her head high and walked away.

Rebel didn't watch her go. She felt strangely disconnected from the whole scene. Not part of her life at all. It was Hugh's life. Cynthia's life. And things that had meaning to them had no meaning to her.

She felt a little stirring of gladness that her grandfather had renounced his title. It was a measure of his love for the mother of her mother that he should turn his back on so much. A measure of his grief at losing his daughter. Her grandparents weren't really strangers at all. They were people like her, who counted love above everything else. She would go and see them soon, reach out to them, make them part of her family.

The oak door of the drawing room closed with a resounding thump. Exit Cynthia, Rebel thought with satisfaction. At least Hugh wouldn't be marrying *her!*

"Why did you sit there saying nothing, Rebel?" Hugh demanded, the rasp of seething anger still in his voice. "Why did you sit there meekly letting that bitch walk all over you? Why weren't you fighting her?"

His voice was coming closer and closer. Rebel pushed herself out of the armchair and swung slowly around to face him. He stopped in his tracks, a metre or so away from her, the dark eyes searching her still pale face as turbulent emotions warred over his. The space between them was barely a pace or two, yet Rebel felt as though she was watching him from a great distance, an unbridgeable distance.

"Why?" he demanded again. "You fought me tooth and nail. You fought Celeste with a psychological skill that would shame a professional. You couldn't have believed in what Cynthia was saying, so why not fight her?"

"What with, Hugh?" Rebel asked bleakly. "I didn't know about my grandfather's lineage. Not that I would have used it if I had known. It's irrelevant to what I am. As for the rest . . ." She gave him a wry little smile. "You defended me beautifully. Thank you."

He frowned, shooting her a sharp look from half-lidded eyes. "You could have told her that I'd offered marriage to you."

Rebel stared at him, totally blank-eyed until she recollected the flippant proposal he'd tossed at her over dinner. A hard, almost unnegotiable lump formed in her throat. "You didn't mean it," she whispered huskily.

The dark eyes seared hers with burning intensity. "You believe her, don't you? You believe that I'd only ever want you in my bed!"

She felt as though he had punched the words at her. Her stomach contracted. She fought to catch some breath. Tears welled into her eyes. She just couldn't find the strength to cope with any more. She shook her head and tried to step past him.

"Rebel!" He grabbed her, swung her towards him, muttered a savage oath under his breath. "Look at me, damn it! Look at me!"

He lifted one hand to cup her chin and force her face up to his.

"I wanted to mean it, Rebel," he said in a tight, hoarse voice. "But what decent man could ask you to share the hell I expected to go through with Celeste? To watch you being hurt and twisted around and your faith in love being ground into bitter ashes? I couldn't do it to you. Do you understand? I couldn't take what I wanted at the cost of dragging you into that black hole with me."

His hand released her face and raked agitatedly through the tangled curls above her ear. "Then yesterday... Yesterday you wouldn't go and you wouldn't give up and I..." He jerked his head from side to side in tortured recollection. "Yes, I wanted to take anything I could have of you for as long as I could... Away from Celeste, away from the evil I saw in her. But, Rebel..."

He dragged in a deep breath, and the glitter of need in his eyes penetrated the film of tears in hers. "If I could have asked you to be my wife with any honour at all, I would have. And last night I thought you were giving me a chance to start again. I meant to court you. To show you a different man, one you might begin to see as a man you could love. A man you'd want to have your children by and share your life with.

That's what I want, Rebel. More than anything else in the world, that's what I want."

The desperate fervour in his voice shook the doubts from her mind. "It's what I want, too," she whispered, barely able to believe that he truly felt what she felt.

He shut his eyes tight. The hand in her hair clenched. He took a couple of short, gasping breaths, then opened his eyes again. "Please...will you say that again, Rebel?" he asked gruffly.

She lifted her hands to his chest and tentatively slid them up to his shoulders as she swayed closer to him. "I love you," she said, smiling tremulously.

He swept her into a fierce embrace that eloquently expressed the agony and the ecstasy of hearing what he had not dared hope to hear. "How can you love me?" he groaned. "No, don't answer that. I swear I'll earn it. I'll spend the rest of my life earning it. So long as you never walk out of it, Rebel."

A shudder ran through him, and then he was tilting her head back, his mouth seeking hers, kissing her with a passion that seemed to draw on the very essence of her soul. A wild, exultant joy poured into her response and rippled through her body as she felt the stirring of his urgent desire for her. Freed of any inhibitions, Rebel's hand swept up. She ran her fingers through his thick black hair as she arched her body closer to his, revelling in the firm pressure of his chest against the soft swell of her breasts, thrilling to the hardness of his arousal. His hands moved over her, feverishly possessive.

Neither of them heard the knock that preceded the opening of the drawing room door, nor saw the child who stood there, watching them with intense interest, a ball of contented fluff nursed in her arms. Finally the need to know got the better of her.

"Uncle Hugh? Does this mean what we talked about?"

Reluctantly he lifted his mouth away from Rebel's, breathed in hard and flashed a look at his niece. "Not now, Celeste. I've still got to get Rebel to fix a wedding date."

"Did she say she'd marry you?" This asked in incredulous delight.

"Just about. I'm working on it."

"You know, Uncle Hugh, you're a lot smarter than I thought." This said with true admiration.

"I'm a *very* fast learner, Celeste. Now go play with your dog until I've got everything settled."

The door closed with a high-spirited slam and there was a loud "Whoopee!" yelled on the other side of it.

Hugh heaved a deep sigh as he looked at Rebel's widely questioning eyes. "If you start thinking I just want you for Celeste, Rebel Griffith James, I'll drag you up to my bedroom and comprehensively drive any such thoughts from your mind. She did a lot of hinting about adoption and mothers this morning. And didn't I think you were beautiful and wouldn't it be nice to keep you at Davenport Hall forever? With which I heartily agreed. In fact, we were in perfect accord on the matter. But I thought of it first. And if you don't believe me . . ."

He set about convincing her in no uncertain manner. He didn't precisely drag her up to his bedroom, but in between some very satisfying and exhilarating lovemaking, Rebel agreed to marry him after the balloon race, and Hugh declared he would fly all the James family to England for the wedding, since traditionally the earls of Stanthorpe always married in the village church.

When they finally emerged from the drawing room, a beaming Brooks informed them that Lady Celeste had taken her new pup for a walk in the grounds. He opened the front door for them, and they strolled out into the midday sunshine.

Life was suddenly full of wonderful promises to Rebel. She hugged Hugh's arm as they descended the steps. "Let's walk down the avenue to the gateway."

Hugh smiled indulgently, his dark eyes glowing with the love he had vowed for all eternity. "I doubt Celeste would have taken that direction."

"I know. But it won't take long. I just want to feel if it's the same."

Hugh threw her a quizzical look, but he followed.

"Have you ever felt a sense of timelessness here?" she asked, looking up at the ancient trees as they passed underneath, dappled sunshine adding its magical patterns of light. "As if the past and the present and future all exist, shimmering around us, and with a blink of an eyelid, all of them could be now."

Hugh smiled at her. "A fanciful idea."

She smiled back. "Yes. I suppose it is."

But it was true, she thought. Yesterday, today, tomorrow... This avenue had led to all of them, as intertwined as the leaves and branches overhead. It was only a few days since she had first walked down here, but so much had been packed into those few days it might have been an eternity. And how could one measure feelings? They just were, regardless of any other reality.

"I do know what you mean, though," Hugh murmured. "Sometimes I've felt oppressed by the sense of long continuity. Other times it's been comforting, to be a part of something that began long ago."

My mother walked down this avenue, Rebel thought, seeing Davenport Hall and being drawn to see more, know more. She was happy here, Valerie Griffith. I'll be happy here, too, Mother, Rebel silently promised her.

Hugh stopped and gently took her in his arms, his dark eyes soft with a deep tenderness. "Now it will go on. I'm not lost to this world any more because of you, Rebel. We were both lost, Celeste and I. And your grandparents as well. But for your giving heart we would have stayed lost. Fate smiled on all of us the day you came to Davenport Hall."

"You don't believe in fate," she reminded him.

"This was the time, this was the place... and you stepped into it. A Rebel with a cause." He smiled and looked at the huge, centuries-old mansion. "I think Davenport Hall was waiting for you to bring it alive again."

"There will be children." Rebel happily envisaged how it was going to be. "And a lot of laughter."

Hugh's arm tightened possessively around her. "Our children. And any lost waifs you decide need adopting. We've got plenty of rooms to fill here. You can have as big a family as you want, Rebel."

"You wouldn't mind?"

"What you want, I want," he replied with heart-warming simplicity, and she loved him all the more for his generosity.

Her very own family, Rebel thought. A new beginning, a line that stretched back into the past and forward to the future. It was a good feeling, the feeling of belonging.